THE PAIN TREE

ALSO BY OLIVE SENIOR

Fiction
Summer Lightning
Arrival of the Snake-Woman
Discerner of Hearts
Dancing Lessons

Poetry
Talking of Trees
Gardening in the Tropics
Over the Roofs of the World
Shell
Un pipiri m'a Dit / A little bird told me

Non-Fiction
A-Z of Jamaican Heritage
Working Miracles: Women's Lives in the English-speaking Caribbean
Encyclopedia of Jamaican Heritage
Dying to Better Themselves: West Indians and the Building of the Panama Canal

OLIVE SENIOR

THE PAIN TREE

STORIES

PEEPAL TREE

First published in Canada in 2015
Cormorant Books Inc.
10 St. Mary Street,
Suite 615,
Toronto
Ontario M4Y 1P9

This UK and Caribbean edition published in 2017
Peepal Tree Press Ltd
17 King's Avenue
Leeds LS6 1QS
England

This edition not for sale in Canada and the USA

© 2015, 2017 Olive Senior

ISBN13: 9781845233488

Supported using public funding by
**ARTS COUNCIL
ENGLAND**

CONTENTS

THE PAIN TREE

1

The person who took care of me as a child was a woman named Larissa. The moment I arrived home, I had a vision of her, instead of my mother, standing by the front steps waiting to greet me with a gift in her hand. It startled me; though she no longer worked for my family, and it had been many years since I'd thought of her, it seemed so real. Suddenly I was a child again, so palpable was her presence. What I'd remembered were the good times we'd had together; it made me feel sad and I didn't know why. I felt cheated of the gift she hadn't delivered, though I knew that to be absurd. Larissa was a poor woman, with nothing to give.

My mother loved to say I was coming home to possess my inheritance. She wrote it like that in her letters. She also told people I'd chosen to study archaeology because I'd been born in a house with seventeenth-century foundations. Yes, I would say to myself, built of the finest cut stone, the mortar hard as iron because it was sweetened with molasses and slave blood. My mother would have been extremely mortified if she'd heard me say that aloud. For us, the past was a condensed version.

I didn't want to possess anything.

When my parents sent me away to boarding school in England at the age of ten, I had happily gone, and managed to stay away for fifteen years. But coming home now seemed the right thing since my father died and my mother was left alone. I was their only child.

2

I had never given much thought to the life I was born into, and duty was something new to me. For the first few weeks after my return I fell into whatever my mother had planned for me, trying to get my bearings, but I had no real sense of connecting with anyone or anything; life here seemed so untouched by the changes in the world. My mother kept talking of what a grand opportunity I had for building up the estate to the grandeur it once had, but all I could think of was how much there was I had to break down. I was already feeling suffocated, only now realizing how often in my childhood I had escaped to Larissa.

"Is anyone living in Larissa's old room?" I asked my mother at breakfast one day.

"Of course not, dear. None of these girls want live-in jobs anymore. They're all day workers. Just wait till this country gets the so-called Independence they're all clamouring for. Then there'll be nobody to work for us at all."

She said this with such petulance that I almost laughed. I looked hard at her, at her impeccably made-up face, even at breakfast, her polished nails and her hair. "Well-preserved" is the way one would have described her. I thought irreverently that that is perhaps why I had studied archaeology. My mother, the well-preserved. Carefully layered. The way she had always looked. The way she would look in her grave. I saw nothing of myself in her, in this house, in this life. But then, I saw nothing of myself anywhere.

3

One day, I left the house and walked down the slope to the old slave barracks hidden behind the trees.

In my childhood, the barracks were used for storage, except for a few rooms that housed the people who worked in the great house. As I neared, I could see the buildings were abandoned, maidenhair fern and wild fig sprouting from every crack, the roof beginning to cave in.

I had no difficulty identifying Larissa's from the long line of doors. I threw open the window as soon as I entered the room, but the light that streamed in barely penetrated the dust and cobweb, so I went outside and broke off a tree branch and used it to brush some away.

The old iron bed was still there – without a mattress – as well as the washstand, the small table and battered wooden chair. I sat on the chair, as I often did when I was a child, and looked keenly at the walls, which were completely covered with pages and pictures cut out of newspapers and magazines and pasted down, all now faded and peeling. This is a part of me, I thought with surprise, for I recognized many of the pictures as those I had helped Larissa to cut out. I got the feeling nothing new had been added since I left.

I used to help Larissa make the paste from cassava starch, but the job of sticking the pictures to the wall was hers alone. I brought the newspapers and magazines my parents were done with, and we looked at the pictures together and argued. I liked scenes of far-off lands and old buildings best while her favourites were the Holy Family, the British Royal Family and beautiful clothes. But, as time went on, headlines, scenes, whole pages about the War in Europe took over, and Larissa wanted me to read all the news to her before she fell to with scissors and paste. With the rapidly changing events, even Jesus got pasted over.

The newspaper pages had looked so fresh when we put them up, the ink so black and startling, headlines imposing on the room names and images that were heavy and ponderous like tolling bells: Dun-kirk, Stalin-grad, Roose-velt, Church-ill. And the most important one, the one facing Larissa's bed with the caption above it saying: "The Contingent Embarking." Larissa and I had spent countless hours searching that picture in vain; trying to find – among the hundreds of young men on the deck of the ship, to decipher from the black dots composing the picture – the faces of her two sons.

It was I, then about eight years old, who had signed for and brought the telegram to Larissa.

The moment she saw what was in my hand she said, "Wait, make me sit down," even though she was already sitting on the steps outside the barracks. She got up and slowly walked into her room, took off her apron, straightened her cap, sat on the bed and smoothed down her dress, her back straight. I stood in the doorway and read the message. Her youngest son was on a ship that went down. I remember being struck by the phrase, "All hands."

I never met Larissa's sons; they were raised by her mother someplace else, but she talked of them constantly – especially the youngest whose name was Zebedee. When the war came, both Moses and Zebedee, like ten thousand other young men, had rushed off to join the Contingents. So far as I know, Moses was never heard from again, even after the war ended.

I can still see myself reading to Larissa about the loss of Zebedee Breeze. "All hands. All hands," kept echoing in my head.

Larissa didn't cry. She sat, staring silently at the pictures that covered the walls to a significant depth; the layers represented not just the many years of her own occupancy, but those of the nameless other women who had passed through that room.

I went to sit very close beside her on the bed. She put her arm around me. We sat like that for a long time. I wanted to speak, but my mouth felt very dry. I could hardly get the words out. "He, Zebedee, was a hero," was all I could think of saying.

Larissa hugged me tightly with both hands, then pulled away and resumed staring at the wall. She did it with such intensity, it was as if she expected all the images to fly together and coalesce, finally, into one grand design, to signify something meaningful.

"Zebedee Breeze," I said to myself, over and over, and his name was like a light wind passing. How could he have drowned?

After a while, Larissa got up and washed her face, straightened her clothes, and walked with me back to the house to resume her duties. My parents must have spoken to her, but she took no time off. I didn't see her cry that day or any other. She never mentioned her sons.

And something comes to me now that would never have occurred to me then: how when the son of one of my parents' friends had died, his mother had been treated so tenderly by everyone, the drama of his illness and death freely shared, the funeral a community event. That mother had worn full black for a year to underline her grief and cried often into her white lace handkerchief, which made us all want to cry with her.

Women like Larissa, pulled far from their homes and families by the promise of work, were not expected to grieve; their sorrow, like their true selves, remaining muted and hidden. Alone in countless little rooms like the one in which I was sitting, they had papered over the layers, smoothed down the edges, till the flat and unreflective surface mirrored the selves they showed to us, the people who employed them.

Was that why we had come to believe that people like Larissa, people who were not us, had no feelings?

I was suddenly flooded with the shame of a memory that I had long hidden from myself: when I was going off to England, I had left without saying goodbye to Larissa, closest companion for my first ten years.

I can see it now. Me: the child with boundless energy, raring to go. Larissa calmly grooming me, re-tying my ribbons, straightening my socks, spinning me around to check that my slip didn't show. Was it just my imagination that she was doing it more slowly than usual? The trunks and suitcases were stowed. My parents were already seated in the car. I was about to get in when Larissa said, "Wait! I forget. I have something for you." And she rushed off.

I stood for a moment or two. No one was hurrying me. But with a child's impatience, I couldn't wait. I got into the car and the driver shut the door.

"Tell Larissa 'bye,'" I shouted out the window to no one in particular.

"Wait! She coming," one of the workers called out, for quite a group had gathered to see us off. But the driver had put the car in gear and we were moving. I didn't even look back.

I had planned to write to Larissa, but never did. For a few years I sent her my love via letters to my mother and received hers in return, but even that trickled away. I never for one moment wondered what it was she had wanted to give me and turned back for. I had completely forgotten about it, until now.

The thought came, unbidden, that only those who are born rich can afford the luxury of not wanting to own anything. We can try it on as a way of avoiding complicity. But in my heart of hearts I know my inheritance already possesses me.

What Larissa wanted more than anything was the one thing a poor woman could never afford: beautiful clothes.

Sometimes when she and I came to paste new pictures on the wall, we went a little bit crazy and ripped at torn edges with glee, digging deep down into the layers and pulling up old pages that had stuck together, revealing earlier times and treasures.

"Look Larissa," I would cry, and read aloud, "'Full white underskirts with nineteen-inch flounce carrying three insertions of Real Linen Torchon lace three inches wide.' Three inches, Larissa! 'Edging at foot to match. Only ten shillings and six-pence.'"

"Oh Lord," Larissa would say and clap her hands. "Just the thing for me!"

After our laughter subsided, Larissa would carefully lay down her new pictures to cover over what we had ripped up. She did it slowly and carefully but sometimes her hands would pause, as if her thoughts were already travelling.

Now I felt shame, not just for the way I had treated Larissa, but for a whole way of life I had inherited. People who mattered, we believed, resided in the great house. It was we who made history, a series of events unfolding with each generation. And yet, I realized now, it was in this room, Larissa's, that I had first learnt that history is not dates or abstraction but a space where memory becomes layered and textured. What is real is what you carry around inside of you.

4

Meeting the past like this in Larissa's room, I began to feel almost
faint, as if the walls were crawling in towards me, the layers of
fractured images thickening, shrinking the space, absorbing the
light coming through the window and from the open door until
I felt I was inside a tomb surrounded by hieroglyphics: images of
war and the crucified Christ, princesses and movie stars, cowboys
and curly-haired children, pampered cats and dogs, lions and
zebras in zoos, long-haired girls strutting the latest fashions, ads
for beauty creams, toothpaste, and motor cars. Images of people
who were never like the people who had occupied this room.

What had these pictures meant to them, the women who had
lived here? What were they like, really, these women who were
such close witnesses to our lives? Women who were here one day
then going – gone, like Larissa. Leaving no forwarding address
because we had never asked.

5

Larissa's room with its silent layers of sorrow so humbly borne
suffocated me. I had this urge to strip the walls, tear the layers
apart. I felt such rage, I rose and put both hands against the wall
facing me and I pushed, wanting to send it tumbling, all of it. Such
rage that my hands battered at the walls. War! I couldn't stop,
couldn't stop my fingers digging into the layers of paper, gouging
and ripping. This is where these women buried their rage. Here!
I sent huge sheets flying. Here! Half a wall of paper down in one
big clump. Over there! Digging down now, struggling with layers
of centuries, almost falling over as the big pieces came away in my
hands. I couldn't stop scratching at the fragments left behind,
wanting to destroy it all, till my nails were broken to the quick and
bleeding.

6

I came to my senses in that dust-laden room, sobbing loudly and holding clumps of rotting old paper in my hand, fragments flying about, clinging to my hair and clothing, sticking to my nose, my mouth, clogging my throat. I coughed and sneezed and spun around shaking my hair like a mad dog, setting the fragments spinning, joining the dust motes floating in the sunlight streaming in.

What a mess I was.

Ashamed, I summoned up the nerve to look at my handiwork. There were places that could never be stripped, the layers so old they were forever bonded to the walls. In some parts I had managed to strip the walls down to reveal dark ugly stains from centuries of glue and printer's ink and whatever else can stain. The walls were an abstract collage now. No single recognizable image was left. Without meaning to, I had erased the previous occupants.

I felt sick at my behaviour, as if I had committed a desecration. Larissa's room. I had no right.

But the longer I sat in the room, the more I realized it was giving off no disturbing emanations. What I had done had neither added to nor diminished it. The rage had not been the women's but mine. In the wider scheme of things, it was a gesture without meaning. The women like Larissa would always be one step ahead, rooms like this serving only as temporary refuge. They knew, from the history of their mothers and their mothers before them, that they would always move on. To other rooms elsewhere. To raise for a while children not their own who – like their own – would repay them with indifference, ingratitude, or death.

I thought I was taking possession, but the room had already been condemned.

I got up and leaned out the window and was surprised at how fresh and clean the air felt. I offered up my face, my hair, my arms to the wind that was blowing lightly and I closed my eyes so it would wash away the last fragments of paper and cobweb. O Zebedee Breeze! The name of Larissa's son had seemed so magical to me as a child, I had often whispered it to myself, and as I whispered it now, it conjured up the long-forgotten image of Larissa and the pain tree.

7

A few days after I had brought the news of Zebedee's death to Larissa, I saw her walking back and forth in the yard, searching the ground. Finally, she bent and picked something up. Then she took up a stone and walked a little way into the bushes. I was so curious, I followed her, but something told me not to reveal myself.

She stopped when she reached the cedar tree, and I watched as she stood for a good while with her head bent close to the tree and her lips moving as if she were praying. Then she pounded the trunk of the tree with the stone, threw the stone down, and strode off without looking back. When I went and examined the tree, I saw that she had hammered in a nail. I was even more astonished to notice there were many nails hammered right into the trunk.

At first, I sensed that this was something so private I should keep quiet about it. But I couldn't help it, and one day I asked Larissa why she had put the nail into the tree.

"Don't is the pain tree?" she asked in a surprised voice, as if that was something everyone knew.

"What do you mean by 'pain tree'?"

"Eh, where you come from, girl?" Larissa exclaimed. "Don't is the tree you give your pain to?"

I must have looked puzzled still for she took the trouble to explain. "Let us say, Lorraine, I feel a heavy burden, too heavy for me to bear, if I give the nail to the tree and ask it to take my burden from me, is so it go. Then I get relief."

"So you put all those nails in the tree?" I asked, for I could not imagine one person having so much pain.

She looked embarrassed, then she said, "Not all of them. I find some when I come here. That's how I know is a pain tree."

"You mean, other people do this?"

"Of course," she said. "Plenty people do it." Then she paused and said, almost to herself, "What else to do?"

After that, whenever I remembered, I would go and look at the tree, but I never detected new nails. Perhaps if I had been older and wiser I would have interpreted this differently, but at the time I took it to mean that Larissa felt no more pain.

Once or twice, when I was particularly unhappy, I had myself gone to the tree to try and drive a nail in. But I did so without conviction and the magic didn't work for me, the nails bent and never went in properly and I ended up throwing both nail and stone away in disgust.

"Maybe people like you don't need the pain tree," Larissa said after my third try.

It was the only time I ever felt uncomfortable with her.

8

Leaving Larissa's room, I deliberately left the door and window wide open for the breeze to blow through. I went outside and stood on the steps of the barracks to get my bearings, for the landscape had vastly changed. Then I waded into the bushes to look for a cedar. I had decided to try and find the pain tree.

It took me a while. At first I couldn't believe I had found the right tree, for what had been a sapling was now of massive growth, its trunk straight and tall, its canopy high in the air.

I didn't expect to see any nail marks, but I knew they were there. I walked around the tree, looking up until finally, with the sun striking at the right angle – and, yes, it might have been my imagination – I caught a glint of something metallic, and what looked like pockmarks high up on the trunk.

Standing there, gazing upwards, it came to me why Larissa and all those women had kept on giving the tree their pain, like prayers. Because they knew no matter what else happened in their lives, the tree would keep on bearing them up, higher and higher, year after year.

I had the uncomfortable feeling that I should be grieving not for them, but for myself. People like me would always inherit the land, but they were the ones who already possessed the Earth.

Before I went back to the house, I spent a long time searching the ground for a nail. When I found one, I picked up a stone. I went and stood close to the tree and whispered to it, and then I carefully positioned the nail and pounded it with the stone. It went straight in.

MOONLIGHT

I found it hard to sleep with the moon like that, falling through the window and right across my bed. One night I got up and climbed out the window onto our back veranda and, after that, I went walking outside in the yard whenever there was moonlight. For no reason, if anyone had asked. I just felt restless. In my nightgown and bare feet I would wander around the yard and take the night in, gaze at the moon and the heavens full of stars till I could feel myself almost floating away. Then I'd pull myself back to earth and hoist myself up through the window and go back to bed and sleep soundly. I wasn't afraid. At that time I was not afraid. Not of lizards or spiders or ghosts or robbers, of hard sums or long words. Which is probably why my grandmother had ended up calling me "too biggish" and "force ripe" when she visited. "Growing up before her time," I heard her say. But I didn't mind. She'd only started to say that after I said I was too big to sit in her lap, which was true. What would she have said if she saw me climbing out of my window at night? Only Darwin our dog saw me from the back veranda where he slept, but he merely lifted his head with his ears straight up and sniffed to let me know he was there and on the job of guarding our house. Darwin was too dignified to make any unnecessary sound: he only barked at strangers.

One night I was so busy wandering around and gazing upwards I didn't realize I was near to Dorleen's room. I nearly jumped out of my skin when I heard a man's voice inside and Dorleen's voice, saying "No. No," then the man's voice again. I stood still, listening. And I heard the voice again. His voice. My father's. Speaking rough, in a way he never spoke to me or my mother. What was he doing in Dorleen's room? I closed my eyes and held my breath too long. I felt the world turning upside down. I knew I had to get away from there without making a sound. No one should know I walked in the moonlight. I tiptoed to my window and climbed back in, my feet trembling all the while. I shut the window and got into bed and pulled the covers up, over my head, for I was suddenly cold all over, as if I had taken a chill.

Next morning, I looked at my father, sitting at the breakfast table, reading the papers in between taking bites of his bacon and eggs. I looked at Dorleen, softly padding around, barefooted, as she came from the kitchen, bringing our breakfast, pouring our orange juice and my father's coffee, clearing the table, returning to the kitchen. Not speaking unless spoken to. Not showing anything on her face. I looked at my mother. She looked the same as she always did. Peaceful. Not showing anything either.

I began to wonder if I had been dreaming. But that night, and many nights after, I couldn't sleep; I stood by my window for hours, listening and watching. And I saw my father, like a shadow, coming and going between our house and the maid's quarters where Dorleen slept.

Though nobody noticed, I became a different person. I couldn't look at my father without tears springing to my eyes. I couldn't stand looking at my mother in case she saw something I didn't want her to see. I started to look away. I stopped eating because I couldn't swallow anything Dorleen had cooked.

School was out for the summer holidays now and it was just me and them. I watched them. I had nothing better to do. For the first time I wished I had brothers and sisters. But nobody behaved differently as far as I could see, and when there was no moonlight and I couldn't see anything outside, I slept like a log.

When moonlight came again, I didn't feel like going outside. I didn't even go to the window. I wrapped myself in the sheet from head to toe so I couldn't see anything, and suffered from the heat. I wanted to ask my mother to make me heavy drapes to shut out the moonlight. I began to feel fearful, though I wasn't sure why. When next my grandmother came I cried because I fell and scraped my knee and she said, "Don't be such a baby," and I cried again.

One morning I came to the table for breakfast and it was my mother in the kitchen. My father didn't notice anything until my mother came out with the percolator and poured his coffee. He must have seen her white hand instead of Dorleen's black one reaching for his cup and he looked up and asked, "Where's Dorleen, then?"

My mother finished pouring, her hand steady, spilling not a drop, and then she went and turned over her cup, and poured. "I paid her off," she said, standing and holding the percolator. "She's four months pregnant." She placed the percolator on the trivet and sat down.

"Oh really," my father said. I watched as he absent-mindedly poured milk into his coffee, though he normally didn't take milk, liking it black and sweet. My mother saw it, too, but didn't say anything. Then he picked up the sugar bowl and put four teaspoons in. "Did she say who the father is?" he asked as he slowly stirred.

"I didn't ask. I know who the father is," my mother said, and she sipped from her cup. Milk, no sugar. Her voice was the same as always.

"Oh?"

I was looking from one to the other and I caught the quizzical half-smile on my father's face.

"Oh yes," said my mother in the same soft voice. She looked squarely at my father now. "The dog never barked."

My father said nothing then. He gave her a little smile and took his first sip. I expected him to make a face, but he didn't seem to mind the milk. He took up his folded newspaper and started to read. My mother buttered her toast. Nothing more was said. My father finished his breakfast and left for work, kissing my mother on her forehead as usual.

My mother got a new maid. Dorleen was never mentioned again. Life went on as always. But I didn't feel "biggish" anymore.

I wished my grandmother would come so I could sit in her lap and bury my head in her bosom.

SILENT

What endured in him was not the remembrance of noise. Not the shots ricocheting in the small room, not the sound of tearing and splintering, not the aftershocks. What remained was the sudden silence that sucked him in and shut the noise out. Only the day before, his teacher had described the eye of the hurricane: that calm, silent centre in the middle of the storm. That sudden stillness before whoosh, from the other direction, the second, more terrifying wind came bursting through. In the heart of this hurricane, he listened for the terror returning, but heard nothing. Not the crack of the door kicked in again, not his father jumping up and reaching for his gun and falling in the very action, not the blasts, the ripping sounds. He thought, in a wondering kind of way, *So this is what it feels like to be deaf*, and inside this new space, he found himself surprised and glad to learn something new, something he could hold on to.

*

Under the bed, where his mother thrust all three of them, his little brother and sister clutch him so tightly they are like warm glue melting against his back. They do not let go even when he begins to crawl to where he can look and see what is happening. Through the space where the pink chenille bedspread ends, a foot from the rough plank floor, he watches the blood pumping out of his father, creeping ever so slowly towards him. He watches the sneakers of the two men dancing around, tossing the place, searching for something, watches as one comes close and lifts a

corner of the mattress, bends down to look underneath and sees
the bundle of children, his face framed by the metal bedspring in
bars of cruel light. In that sudden glare, Joel knows he should
close his eyes but he cannot. He knows the men; they are part of
his father's posse. After a suffocating moment the man drops the
mattress, and when nothing else happens, Joel can't stop himself,
he has to crawl out farther to see more of the room, to see his
mother.

He sees, first, her toes tightly clenched in her slippers, then as
he pushes his head farther out, her hands rigid at her sides. Pulled
by the tension of her body, his eyes travel up past her arms, and
he sees the gun at her head, her mouth opening and closing. He
quickly retreats, closes his eyes tightly, and waits for that final
shot. No sound comes.

He has no idea how long he lay there clutching Clive and
Jessamine – it could have been days or weeks or years – until he
senses someone crawling under the bed, feels his mother's
trembling as she locks her body onto them tightly, wordlessly.

After a time, his mother's grip loosens. She raises her body and
half turns to face the door as he turns towards her, his chest heavy
inside. She puts her finger to her lips and gives him a look that
means "Stay here" and gets out from under the bed just as the
door bursts in again. Police. He can tell from their boots. His little
brother and sister stay silent; not even a whimper, though he can
smell them for they have soiled themselves. Him, too. But he
knows he needs to be quiet for police are dangerous bad men.
Everyone knows.

He watches as they lower their M16s to poke at the body on
the floor, which the flies and ants have already colonized in the
rising heat. They wipe the congealed blood off their boots on
the small rug Miss Simms, his mother's employer, had given
her at Christmas and which no one in the family is allowed to
touch much less walk on. And though he still can't hear, all his
other senses are heightened; sickness is rising in him from all
the smells, nasty smells from sweaty bodies, dried blood, bodily
waste. As if all the everyday noxious odours of the yard and lane,

the entire neighbourhood, the world, are rising up to stifle the air in the room.

He sees the others arrive, the plainclothes men. The first one leans down to get a good look at the man on the floor; he smiles broadly. Others come in to stare at the body, smile and give each other high-fives, strut around and kick with their sneakers and heavy boots at the furniture and possessions strewn on the floor. He can see his mother shaking her head up and down, opening her mouth, turning and moving her body, gesturing with her hands, moving her feet. They take her outside.

He closes his eyes again and drifts back onto the silent island on which they are marooned under the bed, he and his little brother and sister who are now wide awake but silent, too, both with their thumbs in their mouths, still glued tightly to him. He feels as if they will never again be separated from one another. It is as if they are sealed off, hearing nothing of the clamour outside. Nothing from the tenement yard, from the laneway full of curious people, nothing of the everyday sounds, the screams or shouts or curses, the raucous laughter, the music blasting from every doorway, the motorbikes and cars revving up and down the narrow streets and lanes, the scatter of gunshots that near and far pattern night and day like the barking of the mangy dogs.

Then everything happens at once. His mother pulls them out from under the bed, lifts up the baby, and leads them outside through the silently staring crowd to the bathroom where she washes them off, herself too, while he watches the water run red into the hole in the concrete. She rubs them dry and puts them in clean clothes. A policewoman is helping her to dress Jess and Clive and, next thing, the policewoman is taking Jess and the bag with Jess's things and he and Clive are being pushed into the back of a police car.

"Mama," he tries to speak but nothing comes out. She leans inside the car window and puts her hand on his head in that gentle way he loves. "Is alright Jo-Jo. I come to the station and get you later. Look after your brother and sister for me. You are the man in charge."

He opens his mouth to speak but again nothing comes, as if the bullets had been a hand passing across his mouth to seal it. The policeman shuts the car door and they drive off; his last view is of his mother standing there, surrounded by armed policemen, and TV cameras and the street full of curious people. It was a scene so ordinary and everyday in his neighbourhood; he would usually just push through such a crowd on his way to school, even if the bodies were there in full view, not bothering to look or stop to find out who was the latest victim, the whys or the wherefores. He took it to be the way life was lived. He would hear the details at school anyway; the children were always so full of it, playing out the death scene like actors in some gangster movie – Pi! Pi! Pi! At the sound of gunshots, real or imagined, they threw themselves flat, pressing their bodies to the ground. Now in the back of the police car, Joel feels so far away from the scene, from himself, it is as if none of it existed.

He rouses himself when they come to the police station, fully expecting to be locked up in a cell, but in the reception area they sit him and Clive on a wooden bench against a far wall. The policewoman who had taken Jess inside brings her back, sucking on a bottle; she says something and smiles when she hands her over to him.

Just at that moment, pandemonium breaks out at the station. Armed police in riot gear rush in and out; from their movements, he can tell that radios and walkie-talkies are crackling, the station phones are ringing, voices are raised, orders are barked. All the adults are in a frenzy. The children on the wooden bench press themselves against the wall for safety, and are soon forgotten. After a while, Joel moves Jess off his lap and seats her beside him so Clive who is nodding off can lie on the bench and put his head in his lap. Jess doesn't protest as she normally would. She leans against Joel, who puts his arm around her, wondering if she and Clive have also fallen deaf and dumb.

Joel is dying of thirst. His jeans and t-shirt are soaked from the heat of the day and the clammy bodies of his brother and sister. His sockless feet feel slick and damp and uncomfortable inside his sneakers. He contorts his body so as not to disturb the little ones and lifts up first one foot and then the other to take the shoes off, glad he hadn't done up the laces. They are the same make as the sneakers worn by the men the night before, by the plainclothes detectives – the favoured footwear of all real men, like his father, who'd brought them all new shoes from his last trip to New York, crossing off another thing from his long list of promises – like moving them out of the tenement and into a real house, soon.

Joel remembers how proud he was to wear his new sneakers to school, and at the same time worried that someone would beat him up to steal them. Now they feel like fire consuming his feet. He pulls them off and drops them on the floor, then kicks them hard under the bench. He wriggles his toes. He is dying to lie on the bench and go to sleep. He knows he can't. He has to stay alert. He is the man in charge.

Much later, when things have quietened down at the station, someone notices them. Joel sees the policemen and policewoman looking at them and talking. He wonders where they will take them and if they will shoot them and why his mother hasn't come. He knows she will come, for she has never let him down yet. But when? And if the policemen take them somewhere, how will she find them?

The policewoman comes over and takes them in turn to the washroom, making them use the toilet and wash their hands and faces; talking to them all the while, though he can't make out what she is saying. A policeman takes Jess's bottle and Joel is surprised when he brings it back; he doesn't wait on the policewoman, he takes the baby in his arms to feed her, parading around with her as the other police tease him and laugh. Another policeman comes in with bags from Kentucky Fried. Joel didn't know he was hungry until he catches the smell of chicken and fries. He is pleasantly surprised when the policeman hands a bag each to him and Clive. He didn't know he could get through a large Pepsi so fast.

After this, Clive falls asleep. Joel stays alert, watching out for Jess who the police have taken away into another room. By the time they bring her back, in clean nappies and clutching another full bottle, they have switched on the lights and the little bit of sky he can see outside is darkening. His mother hasn't come and the big policeman in charge is looking at them in a vexed way, talking to the policewoman. Joel knows they are going to move them somewhere or take them back home. But what if his mother isn't there? And the gunmen come back? He is sure they took his father's guns, so he won't have a weapon to defend little Clive and Jessamine.

Then his mother does come in the door, in a rush, followed by a well-dressed lady who he knows as Miss Simms, one of the women she did daywork for. Miss Simms is young and pretty and rich. She is always sending them presents. She and his mother turn and smile at them; but, when he makes to move, his mother signals for him to stay where he is. They talk to the police. Next thing, the police rush them all through the back entrance and into Miss Simms' car, which is parked in the lane, and she drives away in a tearing hurry, not in the direction of home. His mother and Miss Simms don't say a word until they are well out of their part of town – a part that people like Miss Simms never visit.

In the back seat, the three of them sit down low as their mother instructs them, so they can't be seen. She herself is crouched down in the front seat so it looks like Miss Simms is the only one in the car. They travel for a good long time like this before their mother sits up and Joel passes Jess over to her.

After that it is as if Miss Simms, with her long wavy hair and thin brown hands on the wheel, cannot stop driving, as if she is the one that has to carry on, carry them far away from the danger that stalks them, through streets Joel has never seen, past gardens and trees and houses as big as churches, way past where Miss Simms lives. They climb higher and higher towards the mountains he sees in the distance, leaving the city far behind. Through the open windows he feels a fresh breeze, air that is cleaner than anything he has felt in his life. Around them, the land is dark, except for the light now and then of a house in the distance, the occasional car headlights suddenly lancing the night, approaching like monsters before abandoning them to the dark. He has never seen such darkness before, yet he isn't afraid. He is kneeling on the back seat so he can look out the rear window and wriggle his bare toes. From this vantage point, he can monitor the splendour of the dark hills that are closing ranks behind them like guards; witness the purity of the clear skies above, and the embedded stars that are shimmering and pulsing like gunshots – but far, far away. And silent.

A FATHER LIKE THAT

Well I never know I would make it back much less get in without
Matron seeing me and cutting my tail for being outside without
permission. Bread and water for a week. Plus, if she ever find out
about the commotion I just cause! But I was lucky, for as soon
as I reach up to the house I could tell from all the noise Matron
wasn't there, for the girls only carry on like that when she turn
her back, leave poor Aunt in charge. So I change into my house
dress and I get inside without a soul see me. But my heart was
still in my mouth from the running and the fright so that if
anybody did say one word to me that evening, I would just start
to bawl. Then I would let my mouth run away with me and tell
them everything. Then dog would nyam my supper for Matron
bound to hear.

But Saturday evening is the only time they leave you alone to
read or play games or watch television and nobody to bother you
except you're on kitchen duty. So by the time I reach the TV room
I'm feeling okay, not like how I was feeling when I throw up all
over the stush lady carpet.

I still wish I could tell somebody. Even Aunt, though I don't
know how Aunt would take it. Aunt sort of nervous all the time.
Ronda Levine say is because Miss Richards – that is Aunt real
name – Miss Richards don't have man and she need a good – well,
you know. I can't bring myself to say it though I'm practising to
say all these things like Ronda Levine and not turn red. Matron
wash out Ronda Levine mouth with soap umpteen times and I
never have my mouth wash with brown soap yet.

Aunt is the one start the whole thing, about how this man is my father though now I have to wonder. But a big person like Aunt would make up something like that? In my heart of hearts I hope it don't go so, for I never want to be family to any of those people.

Aunt is not my real aunt. I call her by her rightful name Miss Richards when anybody else is around, for is not everything you must let people know about you. But when is me and her alone, I call her Aunt because I know her long time and I don't have nobody else. That don't mean she go easy on me, she beat and punish me same as everybody, for Aunt don't joke.

Aunt is Matron assistant, the one that live with her when the rest of the staff gone home. And is because she know my mother that I get into Demercado Home for even though it is suppose to be for orphans and homeless girls, they don't take in just any and everybody there, I can tell you. So by rights I should be in Maxfield Park or Eventide or Nathans Home like all the other poor people pikni. I hear they give you rat to eat at Nathans Home and wee-wee to drink at Eventide. Dress you in flour bag. And sleep you four to a bed. Plus the chink. So I glad I end up at Demercado and have my own bed without chink because I would hate to sleep with anybody else, especially that Eppy Grant who moan and groan and toss and turn every night as if cotton-tree duppy riding her.

★

So I grateful to Aunt, and the house not bad. A big mansion, three storey, that old man Demercado die and leave. Though how one family could live in a house so big that thirty of us and Matron and Aunt living there now quite comfortable thank you is beyond me. But is so rich people stay. Rich people always dying and leaving money for Demercado Home though I wish they could come back sometime and see what Matron doing with it; they would cry the living eye-water to see what she feeding us. And I wish one of them would leave us some money to get a new television set because this old one is giving me eye strain.

Is my mother ask Aunt to ask Matron to take me and since Aunt working here from the year one, Matron agree. So Aunt tell me, for she and my mother like sister from the time the two of them born and grow in the same district in Clarendon and come to Kingston on the same bus. Aunt get the job at Demercado Home the minute she arrive and she still here for she's the steady sort. That's what she always saying. "Beauty is as beauty does, Reema. But it's the steady sort that makes the world go round."

Aunt always say "Beauty is as beauty does" when she talk about my mother and I never know what she mean except I can tell she never like how my mother pretty and glamorous because Aunt not any of those things. She never like the kind of life my mother was leading. No good could come of it, Aunt says, though I was too small to remember what kind of life. Well, one time my mother had a job in one of Mister Canaan store and I don't know what happen, but Mister Canaan is well and truly my father. So Aunt tell me one day and my mouth drop open, for though I name Canaan, I think my mother did get it off a shopping bag. For you can't go anywhere like into a supermarket or the ten biggest store in town, or go to buy hardware or do a hundred other things in life, and don't come out without a bag with Canaan name on it.

By the time I born my mother living with Uncle Nelson so I think Uncle Nelson was my father. But no, Aunt say is because of Uncle Nelson why my mother gone and leave me, for Uncle Nelson get green card for America and when he go there he send for her, but say she have to come without the baby for he never want to mind another man pikni. Especially not one with brown skin. So Aunt tell me.

At least I have Aunt and I know my mother, not like some of those other girls like Eppy Grant who they find wrap up in paper bag at Coronation Market. Can't even say they come from this place or that. Can't say they related to a soul. Still, my mother didn't have to treat me that way, because the day she leave me at Demercado Home she say she coming right back. That I should stay with Aunt and be a good girl and she come back soon and bring sweetie for me. I definitely remember that. So I really think she was coming back. Is only when I grow big that Aunt tell me my mother never plan to come back, my mother never even write to hear how I growing, never send her an address from the day she leave. Is only then I realize my mother trick me in truth. To this day I don't understand how she could lie to me like that. Sometime I think no matter what Aunt say, my mother is going to come back. For Aunt keep telling me to practice speaking nice and not sound butto like the other girls, because my mother always speak nice and dress nice and carry herself nice and that is how she would like to find me when she come back. I try to do all these things Aunt say, though I only have two dresses outside my school uniform and sometime I would rather have a dirty mouth like that Ronda Levine so I could curse off Matron whenever she bother me. Maybe even curse my mother off if she ever come back though the Bible say to Honour Thy Father and Mother that thy days may be long... Oh yes, Aunt show me right where it say so, in black and white. But I don't care, for my days here long enough. Sometimes I just praying for the day to end so I can lie in my bed, by my own self, with nobody bossing me around. And maybe since my mother leave me here and gone about her business, cussing is what she deserve.

Ermalinda curse her own mother sometime, but only when she really vex and in punishment and crying for her mother gone and dead and that is why she cursing her. Ronda Levine say that Matron letting Ermalinda stay because every weekend Ermalinda father come and carry Matron to market in his taxi and she don't have to pay him because he getting payment some other way. When I ask Ronda Levine what other way, she do something – screwing her finger around in the middle of her other hand and she laugh, but she won't tell me what it mean. Ronda Levine is worse than Ermalinda. Her own mother carry her to the judge and beg him to lock her up, she so unmanageable. Since she come here, she don't mess with Matron, for Matron not afraid to cut her tail. For Aunt sake, I trying hard not to follow Ronda Levine too much and to keep myself nice in case my mother decide to come back for me.

The father thing is different because is not like I ever feel I have a father except for that Uncle Nelson and I sorry now I ever have good feelings for him. After Aunt tell me this big important man Mister Canaan is my father, I never tell a soul, for here I am like poor-ting-pikni sitting in Demercado Home and I don't want people have me as poppyshow. Everybody know about my father. But nobody know about me. That he is my father, I mean. I don't know if even he know. Well, I should hope not, for it would be a real disgrace that he never pay me the slightest bit of mind. But I used to look at him on TV and his picture in the newspaper and everything. And I could really see a resemblance. Well, I could see it after Aunt point it out. Aunt keep this big picture of him in her bureau drawer that she cut out of magazine and paste on cardboard and every time I visit her she take it out and make me stand with my face set like how this big man have his, though it don't look natural to me and she start pointing out certain things.

"See there, Reema, look at your nose. The living stamp of his. Those big brown eyes? Look!"

I would look but in truth I think Mister Canaan two eye looking like stale fish. I don't contradict Aunt. I politely agree for she is big woman that know my mother before I born. But I didn't feel no way about this man. He don't mean a thing to me. If he wasn't so rich and important, I would maybe feel different. But I see him the way I would see a movie star or somebody like that, or a rich old person like Mister Demercado who die and leave this house after he and his family finish rattle round in it. Rich people different. They strange can't done.

Well about a year or two after Aunt tell me this big man is my father, he go and die. Not that I cry or anything when I hear it on radio. Is like the Queen die or something. I never feel no way about it, so to this day I could never explain to anybody why, just like that, I decide to go to the funeral. Is like something come over me between the time I'm there wringing out my school blouse over the basin and I move to hang it on the line. It just pop into my head that I should go to the funeral and next thing I rushing round trying to find Matron *Gleaner* so I can see which church the funeral keeping. It's four o'clock on Saturday so I know I can get away easy without anybody see me. I hide my white dress and white socks and patent leather T-strap shoes in a bag behind the big mango tree near the fence and I stand behind the tree and change my clothes and dodge under the fence through the hole Matron don't know about and I reach the road and catch the No. 6 bus that drop me off right in front of the church.

Well there was a big crowd of people everywhere and plenty car but I just squeeze myself through and I see a nice looking lady going into the church by herself, so I walk in like I come with her and take a seat beside her as if I have every right to be there. The lady smile at me so I smile right back. And since I never been to a funeral before, I settle down to enjoy myself. The whole thing come to an end and what happen next is the lady fault, for as we leaving the church she turn to me and she say, "Would you like a lift?"

Well, am I going to turn down a chance to drive in a car? So she tell me her name is Mrs. Henderson and I tell her my name is Marva for that is what pop in my head and she start to talk even before we get into the car and I don't think she stop talk yet. Is like she don't have nobody to talk to, though it hard to understand her sometimes for she talking in this funny way, like when she ask me, "And what is your relationship to the deceased?" I have to think before I figure out is Mister Canaan she talking about, so I tell her my mother used to work for him but she is living in the States and couldn't get to come to the funeral so she say I should go. Well it wasn't a big lie and it satisfy Mrs. Henderson for she don't ask me nothing else, she just keep talking. I paying no attention to what she is saying for I passing through a part of the world I never see before. Is not often we get out of Demercado Home apart from church and school and is the first time I ever drive in the front seat of a car, though is something Ermalinda get to do every week when her father pick her up in his taxi and she never let us forget it. So I am thinking what a pity none of the girls from Demercado Home can see me primpsing off in the front seat of the lady nice new car, looking boasie as if is something I do every day.

I go and see them bury Mister Canaan, and then I think Mrs. Henderson going drive me back to the church or some place that I could get a bus. But she say she is a friend of the family and she going to the Canaan house for a minute to pay her respects and I can come with her and not to worry for afterwards she will drop me at my aunt in Beverly Hills which is where I tell her I living. Well, I was going to pass up a chance like that to see inside his house? Plus I get the feeling Mrs. Henderson kinda lonely and liking my company for everybody else at the funeral come with other people, she's the only lady there alone. All the same I know that once I got there I have to get away from her, so I can get a bus back to Demercado Home. By now, I know dog nyam my supper long time, for it almost night, but I feeling so excited by everything that I don't start to worry about Matron yet and the palam-pam when I get back.

This house is just like Mister Demercado big three-storey house but it clean and pretty, like how rich people house suppose to be. And the garden full of lovely trees and flowers and grass, not like ours which is dirt and bush. Plenty people here too, standing out on the lawn, but I just march in behind the lady and behave as if I am with her, proud that I listen to Aunt and keep myself well and know how to speak properly, not like that Michelle and those other ones who drop their aitches all the time. Some people even hold out their hand and I shake it, but nobody paying me any mind, everybody so busy chatting and drinking you'd think it was a party. Some fellows passing around with trays full of food, not a good hearty meal, little dainty kind of things, but every time one come by I grab as much as I can and stuff myself, for suppertime at Demercado Home gone long time now and Matron going to be so vex, she might starve me for a week.

So I am wandering around the garden and eating and taking it all in and looking at the rich people in their spiffy clothes and thinking how I going to get away so Mrs. Henderson don't see me. And then I find myself standing by the veranda and I look around and not a soul watching so I climb up the steps a little and then a little more till I reach right on the veranda. I go further till

I can peep inside this room for the doors are wide open and this is the most beautiful room I ever seen in my life with carpet on the floor and nice soft furniture you could just fall into and statues and pictures on the wall.

The doors wide open, nobody could say is me open them, so I take a proper look inside and the room is full of all these women in hats, real rich women sitting around and when I look good I realize a lady with her back to me is Mister Canaan wife for I seen her in the church. That make me jump a bit, but nobody notice me, they so busy chatting and eating and drinking, so I walk in and sit on the carpet just inside the door. I really can't tell anybody why I do that, is like a spirit was moving me because the room so pretty, because of the perfume and the ladies in their silk dresses and their hats and their diamonds and gold. I never in my life seen nothing like that, so is like I drinking it all in till I sort of forget myself.

I just wanted was to catch a little bit of that life so I sitting there for a while feeling peaceful. And everything was going fine for nobody notice me except like a spite I have to see something in the room I cannot believe, so I find myself getting up and walking across the room to stare at it, but sort of behind all the chairs and sofas so I'm not in their way. What I get up to look at is this picture in a fancy gold frame. Is a picture of a woman, and she's blue, everything about her blue, even her hair. But the real funny thing is that this woman all chop up. Well, she looking like she get chop up then put back together again, but not quite right and her two eye real funny for one big to everlasting and take up half her face and the other one slipping down the other side and so small you wonder what she could be seeing out of the two of them.

I'm thinking this is a real funny thing for these rich people to have on their wall for right away I know is Delores Stephenson mother that die in the train crash. That's why Delores come to Demercado Home and been acting special ever since for the train crash was the biggest thing that happen and their picture and name in the newspaper and everything, all of those people like Delores mother who get so chop up in the crash they couldn't even fit their body back together. Up to now, they not sure they bury all of Delores mother. Or so everybody at the Home been saying from Delores arrive, which is why ever since we looking at her like she strange to have a mother like that.

So I looking at this picture and thinking why anybody would want a picture of this poor dead woman who get cut up all in pieces by the train on their wall and she dead for sure for her skin and everything is so blue when they could have a picture of a nice bunch of flowers like what Matron have in her office. But then I thinking it can't be Delores mother; what these kind of people would want with her? So the whole thing have me totally confuse.

Matron always telling me my mouth going to get me into trouble one day but sometimes I can't help myself, things just pop out. So I never even know I was saying it loud: "What this picture of Delores dead mother doing on the wall?"

Well, the minute it slip out I wish I could drop through the floor for every woman in that room turn and staring at me with their mouth open and nobody saying a word. I can hear what I say in my loud coarse voice going round and round the room and I know the minute I make the mistake and open my mouth they know right away I not one of them. No matter how nice I keep myself or how nice I look or how nice I try to speak for Aunt's sake. These people just know. For I can't get my tongue around the words soft and round like them, so they know I have no right there and every one of them staring. It's like we're all in a picture, nobody moving.

Then as if to break the spell, this lady, Mister Canaan wife, suddenly jump up and start pointing her finger at me, a fat finger with blood-red nails and full of flashing rings. She get up out of her chair and she shouting: "What is the meaning of this? Where have you come from? Whose child are you?"

I so frighten same time my head swell up big like the time I see the duppy and is like I want to run, but something is holding me to the spot. And suddenly, I couldn't help it, I feeling so sick all the food I been eating just rising to my throat and before I can take a step everything coming up on the lady carpet. That give me a little time to get hold of myself for everybody so shock, they just sitting there and I know Mrs. Caanan stop dead in her tracks. But though I feeling so bad, I not so frighten that I don't see Mrs. Canaan with her long nails coming awake and stepping across the room. And like everything else I been doing I don't know how it happen I just feel my two feet lifting me up and I take off like lightning, out the door and down the veranda steps into the garden and through the crowd of people. I knock a few and even slam into a waiter with a tray but I not stopping for nothing, for I can still hear Mrs. Canaan screaming in my ears, "Who's that child? Catch her, the little devil. Don't let her get away."

But the crowd so noisy I streak off before anybody can take it in and by the time I hear people calling out after me, I gone clear cross the lawn through the gates and right across the street. I hear running and shouting behind me but I don't look for I pelting down the road to the crossroads where I take a right then a left and I running so fast is like I flying and taking the corners as I come to them without paying no attention to where I going. Well I run and I run looking every which way to hide, till I see a place like a park and I cross the road and crawl under a fence and I'm running on grass now, nothing in sight but grass, and I'm flying like a bird, till I come to a wall and I have to stop. Braps!

I cringe up against the wall and try to catch my breath and I look around but I don't see a soul, though that don't mean they not still looking for me and I don't know how much time they give you in prison for throwing up on rich people carpet and nobody to plead for me. I listening out for any sound and then after my heart stop beat so hard I hear this roaring coming from behind the wall and when I listen good, I realize is traffic I hearing. So I look around some more and I know where I am, I'm on the big golf course next to the main road where I get the bus that day. All I can say is Thank God. Thank God, for is like a miracle I know where I am and is not far from Demercado Home. I take a good look round again and I don't see a soul and that frighten me too, for is me one and God out there. But I can't stop to worry now. I look and look till I find a little hole in the fence for every fence must have hole is Ronda Levine motto, for she always running away though she don't escape from Matron yet and I squeeze through and I come out on the main road. By now my nerves really jumpy for I swear I hear people calling out "See her there!" But I don't wait to find out, I start running again as if the devil behind me and I run up the street till I come to the traffic light and it's green so I don't even slow down, I just run through and cross over to the other side and I see the big cotton tree at Demercado Home gate but of course the gate lock to keep everybody in. And my blood is pumping so much I don't even have time to worry about the duppy that living there, I just run past the gate and crawl through the hole in the fence and run straight up to the house.

Mark you I don't show myself right away. I stop and I listen to see if anybody behind me. My heart going boom! boom! so hard that for a long time is only that I hearing. But then it slow down and I know nobody follow me home and I can hear from the noise and confusion coming from inside that Aunt in charge and I'm safe, for she so busy trying to keep order she won't notice nothing. I sit down on the ground for a good long time to collect myself, then I go down to the tree for my house dress and I put it on. Then I realize I better do something about my white dress that I can see have all kind of grass and stain on it. And though it late and I can barely see I know I have to go to the wash house and wash it or I will be in even worse trouble, though everybody know the wash house haunted, but I try not to think of that. I go and wash my dress and I hang it on the line with other people clothes that not dry enough to take in and I know I must remember to come down before day break and check to see if I leave anything for Matron to see.

For a long while after that, I still fretting that those people will find out I come from Demercado Home. I jumpy all the time and I listening out for every car coming up the driveway. But nobody come for me. At first, I couldn't bear to think of what would happen and how I would end up in Eventide or Maxfield Park or even one of those place where they put bad girls for sure. But once I start to relax, and I run the whole thing over in my mind it start to look very funny to me. I have to stop myself from laughing every time I think about it and everybody saying I mad laughing to myself like that, but I can't tell a soul for no matter how much somebody is your best friend today, they will throw everything you tell them back into your face the minute you quarrel.

And I decide I not telling Aunt for Aunt is behaving real strange. A little after the funeral, she call me to her room and hug me, which frighten me for she never do that before, and she say, "Reema I am sorry your father is dead but he was a wicked man and a good thing you never knew him. But I am sure he do right by you in his Will. So Reema, I hope when you are rich you won't forget your poor Aunt who bring you up." And she start to cry.

I never believe a big woman could be so foolish, honest. Is like I am the big people and Aunt the little girl the way she behaving. I almost open my mouth and tell her everything but something tell me no. The way Aunt carrying on, I start to wonder if she make up the whole thing. I wanted was to tell her that if she did see those people at the funeral, she would never think I could be family to them. When I was little maybe I believe something, but now I thinking the whole thing is foolishness. As soon as I leave her that day, I rush to the bathroom to look in the mirror and I'm sure I never see a single thing about myself that look like Mister Canaan. After Aunt carry on like that, I stop worrying about the whole thing because you know what? I'm still feeling so good about how I run away from everybody that night so fast that nobody could catch me.

And that is how it come to me I could beat Ermalinda on sports day. That make me feel so good that when I sit in the TV room the next Saturday night, I forget myself and I give her a cut-eye right to her face because is her big mouth that cause the whole thing, going on all the time about her father. Just because he come to visit her and take her driving in his taxi, Ermalinda always going on about how she not no orphan like the rest of us, though it couldn't be me she calling orphan and how she only there because her mother die and her father soon take her away and who don't have father is cockroach. All this time she there playing with the wristwatch her father give her. All of us vex but nobody answer her for is true plenty girls at Demercado Home don't have father or mother but they don't like to talk about it and nobody else have wristwatch. Ermalinda is such a big-shot at Demercado Home and so own-way I don't think she believe what she see, that I would have the nerve to give her cut-eye right to her face. I could see her blinking her cow-eye and looking at me, but before she say a word I get up and rush outside I laughing so hard. When I come back, I could see Ermalinda looking at me the whole time as if she confuse, but she never say a word to me.

Ee-hee, Miss Ermalinda, I saying to myself now, you just wait till sports day. And that is making me so bold, the next chance I get I find I giving a cut-eye to Ronda Levine of all people, who is bigger than me and the best fighter at Demercado Home and have everybody fraid of her. She beat me up all the time because she jealous I always get my sums right and Matron say that is the only good thing about me, and my handwriting. Ronda don't like how I speak nice neither, but that is only because Aunt beg me. Nobody could say I look for trouble, so normally I would only cut my eye at Ronda behind her back but this time I do it right to her face. Which really surprise me for I never plan it. But she even more surprise than Ermalinda and can't believe I could so bold, for she don't say a word neither, she just keep looking at me all evening. This make me feel badder than ever, so the next chance I get, I not even thinking, I walk straight up to her and give her a shove and she shove me back, hard. I pitch right in and butt her in her stomach so she fall and she come back up and hit me so I see stars but I was ready to hit her back if one of the girls never part us. From the way she looking I could tell that I frighten Ronda for nobody ever fight her back before. So I just give this big smile showing all my teeth right at the moment Matron come to see who making noise and she tell me I lack contrition and punish me worse than she punish Ronda, which not fair for Ronda don't even have to do anything to deserve punishment.

But you know, I never mind because from the time I run like that, and come home by myself past the cotton tree duppy, and go by myself to the wash house to wash out my dress and go out the back in the dark to the clothesline to hang it out, I feel I can take on the whole world.

Every time Ronda look at me, I screw up my face and I saying some bad things, but not out loud. I can tell I'm looking tough, for now Eppy Grant looking at me the way she used to be looking at Ronda, real scared, so I decide I will take on Ronda next time she start to pick on Eppy Grant or the other girls.

The next thing I consider is that since I can run so fast, maybe my real father is somebody who can run fast like those guys you see on TV running in the Olympics. Because you have to get these things from somebody, you know what I mean? Else, how I could suddenly run so fast? I don't think it come from my mother for Aunt say she always dress up in high heels. And that Mister Canaan was fat with plenty cars so he never have to walk, much less run.

But I'm also wondering if my father is somebody who can sing, for I can't carry a tune and Christmas coming and Matron won't have me in the choir, which is wicked, for if you're in the choir you get to dress up and go to all kind of places to sing for rich people and sometime they give you cake and ice cream and I never get to go nowhere. So I'm thinking, as it come to me by accident that I'm a runner, I might find out suddenly that I'm a singer. Boy, what a thing! I'd be the most famous girl in Demercado Home. The fastest runner on sports day and on top of that I would get to go out to sing Christmas carols with the choir. Yea, I bet I have a father like that. He can sing, he can run. Though I don't know.

Sometimes I consider how if I had a real father like that he would be bound to come and find me by now.

I better keep myself quiet and just stick to the running. For next thing you know, at Christmas I going to be standing there in the choir singing away in a church, or the plaza, or even the veranda of some rich people house. And you know what? This rich Mrs. Canaan going to be there. Maybe worse than that we might end up having to go and sing in her very own garden. And just as everything is going good like in the middle of "Silent Night Holy Night All is Calm All is Bright" she going to recognize me and point her fat finger with the rings right in my face and scream: "That's the girl! That's her, the little devil! Whose child is this? Who are you?" And boy, I not lying, if that should ever happen, I swear, this time I would too frighten to run.

No sir, I going to sit and keep myself quiet and concentrate on beating Ermalinda on sports day for nobody big and important ever come to that. Even if my father should turn out to be the greatest singer in the world, and my voice suddenly come so pure and true that Matron herself get down on her knees and is begging me please, please Reema, nobody is going to catch me going out there to sing with any choir.

COAL

Nobody knew what could have made Boy leave the only real home he had ever known. Where, everybody said, he was so well looked after, treated like a king by Sarah and Doll. Who else would have taken in a deaf and dumb boy? Sarah had got tired of correcting people, telling them that Boy wasn't deaf, or dumb, though it was true he didn't speak. But that didn't stop people from calling him Dummy and treating him like an idiot and shouting when they spoke to him.

It was the deaths he had so closely encountered in his short life that made him the way he was, caused him to run away, Sarah said one night out of the blue, as if the thought had just struck her. She lowered the week-old newspaper she was reading aloud from and stared at Doll over her glasses. "I bet you anything something happened inside him when he helped me pull Pops out of the water."

Doll was half-asleep in the old armchair, lulled by Sarah's reading. Jerked awake by the sudden change in tone, she found herself distracted by how much Sarah looked like her mother in the light cast from the Home Sweet Home lamp on the dining table, her beautiful curly hair pulled severely back, her mother's gold-rimmed glasses perched on her nose. *Sarah is turning old before she is even properly a young lady.* This thought came so suddenly to Doll that it brought tears to her eyes and, alarmed at such a thing, she sat up straight and listened to what Sarah was saying. Something about Boy.

"After all, remember he was there alone when his Granny died? A whole day. That poor little boy. And then he was there with his dead Grandfather, too. We never did find out about that."

Doll chupsed in her usual way and sank back into the armchair. She didn't bother to point out that right now the whole world was a dead-house since a quarrel among those white people broke out that she for one didn't understand. "World War," they called it. The Second. There was one before? How these people so stupid?

The fighting was far away, in England and Germany and places like that, and in ships at sea, which was something Doll didn't really understand. But that didn't matter. Boys they knew were over there, fighting; the young men from their district had merrily rushed off to join Contingent when the Big Men came around to ask who would fight for King and Country.

Doll was glad she had no boy children to act so foolish, but she kept her thoughts to herself. War fever had caught hold of everyone, even the rich women who were busy holding knitting bees and giving their jewellery and money to this fund to buy a battleship – or maybe it was an airplane. Doll was disgusted that Sarah had got caught up in the foolishness and had scoured their house and land for metal they were busy collecting for the "war effort". Cho! Doll didn't see the point of getting excited about something you couldn't see or touch, about a king and queen who existed only in pictures in magazines and newspapers. They were so clean and pretty, so well-fed and satisfied that they failed to move Doll. It wasn't like they were doing anything useful like Queen Victoria of her grandfather's time who wore a crown and had held that big thing they called a sceptre in her hand like a club and had roared at the plantation owners, her eyes bulging, "Let my people go." And they had had to comply with her wishes and free the slaves, and go home to England or wherever with their tails between their legs. Now that was ruler! So Doll's grandfather had said. The mightiest the world had ever seen, just like King Solomon the Wise.

She couldn't understand why all the fuss about this wishy-washy looking king, wearing a suit like everyone else, his queen in her pearls, and their two daughters in their shoes and socks and little coats, their hair nicely curled. Not wanting for anything. And look how poor pikni here a bawl for even a drop of milk.

Doll used to say that, but nowadays she kept her mouth shut, for when she had ventured to air those views to Sarah, Sarah had insulted her and told her she fell into a majority of one. So now Doll didn't bother to say to anyone "I told you so" for that would have been wicked when she saw how busy Postmistress and the messenger boy were these days, delivering the black-banded telegrams left and right. This boy dead. That one missing. Doll had gone to so many memorials and set-ups for the dead she was ready to drop from exhaustion. And it wasn't satisfying. How could one hold a wake withouten body, she muttered every time. Then, next thing, Boy had run off too, gone to turn soldier.

Doll wanted the war to be over so they could get saltfish again, and soap, and rice and flour, kerosene oil for the lamps. She found the war tiring; so many things had vanished from the shop shelves, they were busy day and night producing substitutes. She was tired of boiling down oil nut to make castor oil to burn in the lamps. How she longed for some charcoal, but nobody around knew how to burn coal anymore. Not since Coal, Boy's grandfather, had ceased to come around.

It was only now that she had to take on all Boy's chores that she realized how useful he had been, and how she missed his silent presence. Their relationship had see-sawed. Her hitting and cursing him and calling him "Dummy" when he annoyed her was balanced by her indulgences with food, in cutting his hair, looking after his clothes and smoothing down his collar when he dressed for church. When she told him bedtime stories and sang to him in the good times, he became the son she never had. Now she cursed him every time she walked to the spring for water and heaved the kerosene pan onto her head; the drought was so prolonged this year their water tank had run dry. She cursed him as she trekked farther and farther, machete in hand, to slash at any dry branch for firewood, and when she fed the chickens or did other tasks that were his. Mark you, Doll thought as she sank into a doze again, there had been less and less to do in the house since the Master died, for now it was just her and young Sarah – which is how she still thought of her, though Sarah was now a young woman in her twenties.

One good thing Boy's disappearance did was pump life into Sarah again, lifted her from the sorrow into which she had fallen once the funeral was over and they had cleaned out the house and washed all the linens and ironed the Master's clothes and put them aside, as everything usable had now become precious.

After the funeral expenses, there was no money, not even for paying Doll. But Doll had worked for Sarah's family for so long it didn't matter, she had no other home, and she trusted Sarah to put things right when money came in again. Where from, they did not know, but once the war was over and the men returned, they could hire people to work the land again, clean the pastures and get some cows, put it all to good use.

The two often discussed various schemes for money-making, sitting around the dining table after supper was cleared away, with the one lamp they could afford to keep lighted. Sarah would read aloud from the newspaper sent over by their rich neighbours, the news stale but it made no difference, it gave them something to talk about. As she read about the role women were playing in the war, Sarah swallowed the thought that she had been left behind. So many girls her age had left home to volunteer their services, were working in offices and taking the place of men who had gone overseas; some had even been recruited for overseas duty themselves. But she couldn't leave.

Throughout all this, Boy had sat on a stool in the corner, his sharp intelligent eyes darting from one woman to the other as they spoke, taking in everything. Doll's favourite topic was the burning of coal. They talked about how many old, broken-down trees there were on the land that was now Sarah's, how they could make money off it, if only there was someone to build the coal kiln. But all the old coal burners had died off and the young ones had gone for soldiering. Now charcoal, any fuel at all, was as scarce as hen's teeth.

Everyone thought Boy too had run off to join the Contingent, for though they calculated that he could be no more than fourteen, he was big for his age with a mature demeanour. Other overgrown boys that age had got away with lying to recruiters. But they weren't sure the army would take a boy who never spoke a word, though as somebody pointed out, in the army soldiers weren't expected to speak but to do as they were told – and that Boy was good at.

★

Sometime after the funeral, when Sarah felt well enough to rehash with friends and neighbours what had happened, she realized Boy had spoken the day her father drowned.

Early that morning, with the fog barely lifting and the dew still on the grass, Sarah had woken up and discovered that her father was not in his bed or in the house. She had followed his footprints on the wet grass down to the pond, and as she neared it her heart started to swell in her chest until she could hardly breathe or move, her feet already feeling as if she were treading water. She remembered nothing after she caught the flash of blue in the pond, down among the floating water-lily pads. Not her screams, nor her wading into the water to catch hold of the old terry cloth robe and of trying to pull her father out, not her shouting out "Doll, Doll."

Someone had appeared at her side, helping to tug at the body. It wasn't until afterwards that she realized it was Boy. When both of them had pulled her father onto the bank, and the water gushed out of him, she said to Boy, "Go, get help quick. Get Doll," though she knew that her father was already dead. Boy had simply nodded and taken off, water streaming from his pants. He tugged at Doll, who was making up the fire in the kitchen, and pointed in the direction of the pond. Then, running to the neighbours, to the Doctor, and to her friends, the Hallams, who lived in the big house on the hill, Boy had said the same thing: "Come quick. Miss Sarah. The Mister," and had taken off again. By the time the last of them arrived, Boy was back at the scene, silent once more.

When Sarah felt strong enough, and had settled her father's affairs, she remembered how Boy had spoken. She thought that she had never thanked him for what he had done. Although she and Doll had already decided what of her father's things they would save for him, she also wanted to give him a present, a tangible reward. She thought he would like her father's leather wallet, into which she placed a five-shilling note.

She called him into her father's room, where she had placed the wallet on the dresser. He came and stood in front of her, and perhaps it was the way the light struck his face, but he suddenly filled her with wonder, as if she had never really looked at him before. Not seen the bold sculpture of his face, held proudly as an ebony carving, the straightness of his stance, his large, liquid eyes. Even his haphazard haircut, administered by Doll, failed to disguise his beauty.

She had meant to thank him and hand him the wallet, but instead found herself saying in surprise, "Boy! My goodness, how you've grown. You are a big man now. We can't call you 'Boy' anymore!"

She said it in a quizzical way, and caught how Boy lifted his head, his face all aglow and expectant. She found herself floundering, fishing around in her mind for his rightful name, a name she had heard only once when his grandfather had brought the little boy round for the first time.

She remembered how Coal had lifted him down from his perch on top of the crocus bags filled with charcoal.

"And who is this?" she had playfully asked, bending down to smile at the solemn little boy, only his eyes showing white in the grime and coal dust that covered him and his rags.

Coal had proudly said, "Is mi little gran this. Him name —. Say how-di-do to the lady."

Visualizing the scene again, try as she might, she could not remember the name that Coal had said, for after that one instance, it turned out that he himself called the child "Boy" and that is what everyone had taken to calling him. And, long after, when the grandfather died and a stranger brought the child to them, the man had called him "Boy" too, and the boy never spoke. Not his rightful name or anything else.

Now standing there, with the boy still waiting expectantly and her mind a blank, Sarah fought hard to recollect his name, as if it were the most important thing in the world. She focused her mind inwards, and suddenly it popped onto her tongue. "Vincent," she cried in triumph. "Vincent!"

The smile that broke on the boy's face was so radiant that Sarah couldn't help it; she threw her arms around him and hugged tightly. When she released him, she felt her face wet with tears. The boy also had tears in his eyes, but he was smiling, too, as he squared his shoulders and marched from the room. That was the last anyone saw of him.

★

At first they thought he would return. He had taken his machete and other tools, salt from the pantry, but had left his good clothes. The old mule was also gone, the mule that had belonged to Coal, the mule on which the stranger had brought the boy. He had left the mule with them, the boy's only possession, and the mule had grown fat in the pasture. Boy had taken good care of the animal, had ridden it to collect firewood and to the market. Sometimes they had rented it to others, getting paid in kind. Boy spent a lot of time with the mule; from afar it looked as if he talked to it, making sweeping gestures with his arms. Sarah and Doll laughed whenever they caught sight of him; but, try as they might, they could never get close enough to hear without his seeing them, and once he saw them, all gestures ceased.

"A so bwoy pikni stay," Doll pronounced after Boy did not return, and she said it angrily, to hide the betrayal she felt. "Once they think they turn man, they tek off. Have to go feel their own fire. Nuh seven year?"

Yes, Sarah calculated, Boy had been with them for seven years, arriving when he was six or seven. And in all that time she had never attempted to obtain his birth certificate, or find out if his birth was registered, had never given him a proper name, as she had intended when he had first come to live with them.

Perhaps if the teacher had agreed to take him into the school, she would have been forced to go through the process, but when this didn't happen, she had let everything go, caught up with nursing first her mother, then her father, holding the household together.

She felt ashamed now, and sad, and wondered if Vincent knew what his surname was, and if he would give that to the army. Suppose he died, Over There, what a waste that would be. Would they never hear the news for nobody would know who to tell?

There would be no black-edged telegram coming to their house, for now she realized that though she had taken Boy from the stranger without question, she hadn't rightly taken him in. She angrily brushed aside the tears that fell. This was her destiny in life: to lose things, lose everyone that mattered. And now with no life beyond their limited circle, she was beginning to feel she was lost, too.

For some reason that she couldn't fathom, Sarah never told Doll of her last encounter with Boy, though she told her that she remembered his name. She stopped referring to him as Boy for she had started to think of him as Vincent, and soon Doll did too. They reported his disappearance to the District Constable, but, like everyone else, he treated it with scant attention.

"Well," he said, "now you can get a good yard boy to come and help you, two ladies living alone like this. You need more than a Dummy in the yard."

"Dummy" is what Teacher had implied, too, though he hadn't said the word, when Sarah had asked him to take Boy into his school. He said "No" because he would be a disruptive influence, the butt of teasing from the other children, as indeed he was every time he ventured beyond the sphere of those who knew him.

Sarah hadn't pressed the point; she taught Boy at home, giving him the books she had used. It was hard to teach him to read when he wouldn't pronounce the letters, but he had copied the alphabet on his slate and he seemed to have taken in the rudiments of reading and arithmetic. She often caught him looking at the books, at the magazines and newspapers that came to the house, moving his lips silently, but she was never sure how much he could read. That he could speak there was no doubt. He had spoken as a small child, when his grandmother was alive, indeed "chatty-chatty" was the way his grandfather had described him.

The grandfather was known to all and sundry as "Coal" because making and selling charcoal was what he did for a living, a valued occupation in those days when only the rich had woodburning or kerosene stoves, or, rarely, electric. Every few months he would turn up with his rickety mule-drawn cart piled high with dirty crocus bags full of coal for sale by the kerosene pan measure. Sometimes when the big landowners felled trees, they would summon Coal and he would make up his kiln on their property, sleeping rough through the tedious weeks of stacking the wood just so and making it slowly burn down to charcoal.

It was after his wife died that he started carrying his grandson around, for he had nobody to leave the child with. His only son, Charlie, who lived in Kingston, had brought the boy when he was one-year-old and asked his parents to keep him for a while, as its mother had come and dumped the child on him. "Just like that," Charlie said, wondering at the cruelty of the woman, before he himself walked off without a backward glance. That was the last time the old people ever saw or heard from him.

It would have been alright if Miss Mae, his wife, hadn't dropped dead so suddenly, Coal told Sarah. "Dropped dead as she was hanging out the clothes on the line." Coal had come home that evening to find her lying where she had fallen in the yard, stiff as a board and the little boy sitting beside her, his tiny hand holding his grandmother's unyielding one, so tightly that it had taken Coal ages to disengage him. "Oh," the women said in sympathy; but Coal said proudly, "Na, he wasn bawling or nutten." And he rubbed his cracked and coarse hands fondly over the head of the little boy, who was stuck firmly to his side, his two little hands encircling his grandfather's trousered leg. "One tough little man yaso. Nutten to eat all day and sitting there alone, not even moving to brush off the ants and flies. Ants bite him everywhere. Yu shoulda see how him swell up. An him doan cry yet."

When he first started to come by Sarah's house, Doll would take charge of the little boy, scrubbing him down and dressing him in the clothes Sarah had taken to making for him, feeding him and coaxing him into laughing and playing. But he remained silent and shy with them, and as soon as his grandfather reappeared would run to him and hold tight onto the old man.

"Lord, Coal, leave the boy with me, nuh!" Doll would tease him each time he visited.

And the old man would laugh and say, "Next time, Miss Doll." But they knew he would never part with the boy.

The boy went everywhere with Coal. Although at first he was too small to help much, his grandfather explained everything to him as he worked; and though he no longer spoke, it was amazing how quickly he learnt. By the time he was four or five he was a proper little helper. They lived out in the bush for weeks at a time, burning enough coal to make up a load, managing on salt and flour dumplings and roots and wild herbs and the birds his grandfather caught in a springe. They saw no other humans except the occasional hunter or other coal burners.

Once, when he came to burn coal on her father's property, Sarah had ridden into the bush to witness the operation, and was appalled at the amount of work involved. First he had to cut and split the wood, then prepare the ground and build the huge pyramid of wood around a centre pole and chimney, then carefully cover the pyramid with leaves and soil to control the burn. Every aspect required the greatest skill, from the selection of the wood, to the building of the pile with its carefully placed vent holes, to setting it alight. As it burned, the kiln had to be carefully watched day and night to see that no air entered the stack. Once the smoke turned from white to blue, signalling the end of burning, the stack had to be allowed to cool for several days before it could be opened. Even then, there was always the danger of fire flaring up; they had crocus bags of soft earth ready to throw if that happened. Finally, they would rake out the charcoal, Coal listening carefully to the sound that would tell him his product was of the highest quality, hard and brittle, before placing it into the bags and sewing them up. The heat and dirt were unbearable, but the little boy, like a devil's imp, was everywhere, proud servitor to his grandfather.

When a stranger turned up with the boy one day, they didn't need to ask what had happened. Doll installed him in the little room next to hers, and Boy he became to them all. He grew, he thrived; over time, he smiled. He was willing and helpful and attached himself to Sarah's father who was healthy still, but given to forgetfulness and wandering. The little boy took to following the old man around and when they saw how carefully he steered him from danger and brought him back home, the women felt relieved of that added responsibility. It was clear that Boy understood every word that was said and he willingly followed instructions. He never spoke, not until the morning Sarah needed him to speak.

But, she thought wearily after he left, what good was that now?

*

After some months passed, they decided Vincent was just another ungrateful child, one they would never see again. From time to time Sarah went into her father's room, took out the wallet she had put back into the drawer and stroked it, placing the soft leather against her cheek. Sometimes she felt the hot tears gushing down, and she had to dry the wallet on her skirt, never sure if her tears were for Vincent or her father.

The dry season lasted. Doll muttered each time she went in search of wood, muttered each time she lit the wood fire to cook, or boil the clothes, or heat the clothes irons. Muttered that children were worthless and so was the wood – look how fast it burned. Muttered every time she looked at her coal stove in the corner, covered in cobweb, neglected and forlorn. How the good old days were gone, she thought, nobody around to make coal anymore, how this stupid war has changed everything, taken everybody away.

On one of those hot and miserable days, Sarah was sitting in the cool of the veranda, sewing, when she saw the side gate from the laneway slowly open and watched with dread and surprise as an apparition, the ghost of Coal, staggered through. Hand to mouth, she managed an "Oh." Coming through the gate was a mule dragging a makeshift cart, laden down with crocus bags. When the driver went to close the gate the mule stood still, just as Coal had trained his to do. Sarah looked at it and thought it was the same one that had spent so many years in their pasture, though somewhat thinner. Then she decided it couldn't be. This was just some new coal man that was making the rounds, and she knew Doll would be happy if they could buy even one tin.

Her curiosity aroused, she got up and started to walk towards the cart, just as the driver came around to the front. He was ragged and black from head to toe, covered in dirt and coal dust. At first she could see only the whites of his eyes but when he turned and saw her, his face burst into a smile that she would have known anywhere.

"Vincent!" she cried, running toward him.

"Coal, Miss Sarah," Vincent said. His voice stopped her in her tracks. It was unfamiliar and coarse, like a grown man's. "I making coal. Sell in market. Dead wood turn into money. Plenty wood to burn."

By this time Doll had come out to join them and, for a moment, the three of them stood, silent, lost in the sense of something miraculous having occurred – but exactly what that was, none of them would ever be sure.

THE GOODNESS OF MY HEART

1

Everybody knows Mr. Bailiff died with a smile on his face in a well-known house in town, though the newspaper death announcements as well as lengthy obituaries said he had died "peacefully at home, after a brief illness, leaving beloved wife Alicia, prominent social worker." Mr. Bailiff was listed as "successful real estate developer and philanthropist." No mention of children. Of course the rumour mills also ground out that Mr. Bailiff had died in the arms of not one but two or even three ladies of the night (depending on the source) indulging in "unspeakable" or "daring" new sexual acts (depending on whether the teller was man or woman).

Though the location of his passing was correct, Mr. Bailiff had in fact died sitting at the bar having a drink, joking with a few of the other regulars and Linna, the proprietor, relaxed and comfortable as he had been in that very same spot with the very same people for at least twenty-five years. Someone had told a joke, Mr. Bailiff laughed, the laughter turned into what was interpreted as coughing, someone got ready to pat him on the back, then he suddenly spun around on the stool and fell to the floor. Linna, who habitually wore nothing but an upswept hairdo left over from the forties and a flowered kimono (though she was no longer in active practice, so to speak) had enough experience of crises in her establishment to take the matter firmly in hand. Once Mr. Bailiff's demise was established (she held up a mirror to his nose) his body was hastily put into his Benz and driven home by one of his friends, others accompanying him in another car. Mrs. Bailiff was told he had fallen ill and a doctor was summoned, but of course by the time he arrived Mr. Bailiff was stone cold. Judging by the friends who had brought him home (the very ones forbidden from her house so long ago and permanently fixed in her mind as shoe salesman, minor parish council clerk and general ne'er-do-well) and the fact that their hangdog expressions (in Mrs. Bailiff's presence) were even more extreme than usual, Mrs. Bailiff thought it best to ask no questions. No violence had been done to Mr. Bailiff's person that she could see, his expression being so peaceful. The doctor (and family friend) confirmed that Mr. Bailiff had died of a heart attack, which is exactly what Mrs. Bailiff had expected to happen one day, with the life he led. Her own heart she knew was shipshape; she knew how to take care of it.

Mrs. Bailiff spent a long time wondering if she should mention the children in the death notice. There were four of them; all called Bailiff, though none had come from Mrs. Bailiff's body. She had taken them in (or had them thrust on her) as babies, and still referred to them as her "little adopteds", though Ruby the eldest was now the other side of thirty and weighed close to three hundred pounds, and Oral, the second boy who had turned into an almost-Olympic runner, was six feet tall. The other was Christopher, who weighed hardly anything and called himself an artist, and whose height it was hard to judge for he generally kept out of sight and was always hunched over some drawing or other when glimpsed. Finally there was the runt, Elvis, who behaved as if he was eleven feet tall, like the figure in the foreground of a Western shoot-out, the bad guy, someone Mrs. Bailiff tried not to have any thoughts about for fear of contamination from fallout.

Working on the death notice, she told herself it was because of Elvis that she didn't want to list the children. It would look too obvious if she put the others in and left him out. But she was not going to have her name (and that of the late Mr. Bailiff, she hastily tacked on) associated with illegal acts, with someone who was known as Mister Big in drug-dealing circles, who moreover occasionally spent time in Miami jails. Never mind Elvis was said to be the third richest man on the island, after a hurry-come-up hotel magnate and the chairman of a family conglomerate built on a solid base of money dubiously accumulated over centuries but by now washed whiter than snow. Never mind that Elvis had married the beauty-queen daughter of a prominent politician in what was billed by the newspapers as "the wedding of the year". In response to the dictates of her pride, Mrs. Bailiff had stuffed her conscience into her beaded evening bag and attended – but she expected everyone to understand it hadn't meant she endorsed Elvis and his life.

It gave Mrs. Bailiff some satisfaction to think that she had not created Elvis the gangster. He was a problem child from the start, so much so that she would have given him back (she had witnesses to that!) if she had known where to find his mother or even who she was (for that was another story). It was that very mother she blamed for how Elvis had turned out, for what good could come from a child burdened with such a name?

She was only slightly aware that her argument about naming would not hold if she thought of "Oral", a name she loathed more than Elvis (having even less truck with evangelical televised religion than with rock and roll) but she had got Oral too late to make a name change stick (and so had never even tried with Elvis, who came after). Small as Oral was, he had absolutely refused to answer to the name "Michael" which Mrs. Bailiff had selected for him, after the Archangel, instead of what she thought of as a mouthwash. Oral at two was already showing that will of steel that would take him to the height of competitive sports (though of course no one had imagined he would ever amount to anything).

When Mrs. Bailiff thought about it, these children that she had taken into her home had not turned out too badly, all things considered – which is why she spent a lot of time on the wording of the death notice. She actually wrote in the names, putting the word "adopted" before "children", then crossing "adopted" out, then leaving in "children" and crossing out all the names, then doing something else entirely. The whole business took up the entire morning and a good portion of her writing pad as she kept changing her mind. It was uncharacteristic, and showed how upset she really was by Mr. Bailiff 's death. It was only when Griff, who drove for them, came and said he had to go to the newspaper office now or they would never get the notice in for Sunday that she finally made up her mind. Or rather it was Tidie who made up her mind for her, as Tidie had done for the last thirty-odd years.

Tidie was Mrs. Bailiff 's domestic helper and confidante and general adviser. Tidie, who was never called by her real name – Maud Griffiths – had come as a young girl to work with the Bailiffs. While many other domestics had come and gone, she had become entrenched, living on the premises with her son, Griff. By the time she had Griff, Mrs. Bailiff had come to depend on her so much she actually allowed her to come back with the baby, and with the other children arriving, Griff fit right in, like another son of the family. Tidie had no more children, but was kept busy taking care of the "little adopteds" and came to be regarded as more of a surrogate mother than Mrs. Bailiff herself. Mrs. Bailiff had no qualms now about calling Tidie in to consult about the important matter of whether or not the children should be listed in the death notice. Tidie had no reservations at all. "No," she said firmly. Mrs. Bailiff, who was used to Tidie's cut-and-dried manner, was startled at how definite she was. She found it so curious that even as she crossed out not just the names but accidentally (she was to say later when Ruby cried about it) all references to children on the notice, she asked, "Why you say so, Tidie?"

Tidie said in her direct way: "Because, Miss Alicia, is not a good thing to name them. Suppose you was to find out there is more?"

"What?" Now it was Mrs. Bailiff 's turn to be startled. She looked at Tidie, who stood in the doorway leaning against the doorjamb with her arms folded across her chest, giving Mrs. Bailiff what she could only interpret as a cool stare. Nobody else in the world could look at Mrs. Bailiff like that and get away with it, but she put up with a lot from Tidie, as she was the only one she felt already knew her secrets and so had to be trusted. Tidie, as far as Mrs. Bailiff knew, was dedicated to her and the children, having no friends that she could see, was entirely honest and kept the house running in an admirable way, leaving Mrs. Bailiff free for her charitable pursuits. As time went by, Mrs. Bailiff had taken on more and more of organizing just about everything in the town – her "social work" (for those were the days when people were still willing to allow themselves to be organized by people like her). The only thing she had against Tidie was her son Griff, whom Mrs. Bailiff always thought was up to no good though she had never been able to get the slightest bit of evidence of any wrong-doing. Griff in fact had turned out to be as useful to the family as his mother, doing the driving when necessary, running errands, being Mr. Fix-It around the house, having rejected most schooling to become part of the indispensable machinery of the Bailiff enterprises. Mrs. Bailiff frequently thought of her animosity towards Griff (that she took care not to show) because she did not understand its source. He had done nothing to provoke it, except that she had always found him lacking in the kind of respect she expected from a boy who was, after all, no more than the maid's son. Griff's casual manner came, she knew, from his having grown up as one with the other children, so he felt in a way that he, too, was a child of the family. All these thoughts ran through Mrs. Bailiff's mind unbidden now, when she really should have been contemplating what Tidie had said. One thing she had learnt since childhood was to think carefully before speaking. She needed to think carefully, for she was stunned by the suggestion that there might be more children of Mr. Bailiff out there. More than the four she had managed to corral and raise as their own? It was unthinkable. He had said no when she asked, though that had been many, many years ago. But after Elvis, no more children had been left on their doorstep, though if truth be told that was after Mrs. Bailiff had spread the word throughout the town – via Tidie – that she would tolerate no more foundlings, and all in the future would simply be forwarded to the police station. So great was the power of Mrs. Bailiff that by that time, no one dared to test her. "Tidie," Mrs. Bailiff said sternly now, "Are you trying to tell me something? Do you know something I don't know?"

Tidie was twisting the end of her apron – a sure sign of discomfort, Mrs. Bailiff knew. But she was not giving anything away. "No, is not that I know anything... I just wondering... well you know the Mister..." she said, letting her voice trail off.

Mrs. Bailiff let out a huge sigh of relief. "Well," she said sharply, "you should do better than wonder such a thing." Feeling she had probably been too harsh, she said in a nicer voice, "If there were any more of his children out there, don't you think we would know by now?" Mrs. Bailiff said "we" for she had come to include Tidie in such affairs. She had also thought for a long time that her husband (who had died in his early seventies) was probably past what she considered the child-producing stage. Tidie said nothing, just gave her little half-smile and left to call Griff to come for the envelope to take to the newspaper.

2

The first time Tidie had snagged Mrs. Bailiff's confidence, it was at a stage in her marriage where she had given up hope of ever having children of her own and had taken the step of banishing Mr. Bailiff from bed and bedroom (not that he had spent much time in either). By then she had learnt of his ramgoating, unconsciously using the same word her own mother had used for a father whom she had never known. For all his newfound respectability – cemented by business success, philanthropic gestures and by his wife's dignified public bearing – Mr. Bailiff had not changed his low-life habits, and still loved rum bars and whorehouses. She thought she had successfully chased away his old friends, but now, the newest insult had reached her ears: rumours of a child.

It was Tidie who had brought her the news (the means by which all news of that nature was brought, for Mrs. Bailiff cultivated no other confidantes). Tidie, who never left home except to go to market once a week, was nevertheless up-to-date on every piece of gossip in town, especially as it pertained to the "Mister", as she persisted in calling the man of the house. That day, she had stood in front of Mrs. Bailiff, and with eyes downcast and much twisting of her apron, said she had something to tell her. Mrs. Bailiff was not to get vexed; she was only telling her because ol' nayga had it outa street and she thought Miss Alicia – who was so good to her – should know. With Mrs. Bailiff's encouragement she finally blurted out, "One dutty gal outa street call Mirabel say she have baby for the Mister and she going to bring it right up to you one day when you there at yu meeting, looking crips in your nice iron clothes an'ting, or coming outta church with yu hat and purse and shoes matching or someplace stush like that, and she going to hand the baby right over to you, then and there, in front of the whole town."

"What!" Mrs. Bailiff was more shocked at the horror of being confronted by a street girl in a public place than with the idea of Mr. Bailiff fathering a child, for that latter event she had always considered within the realm of possibility, knowing his ways and having determined that the fault in her failure to bear children was her own.

After her initial shock at the news, Mrs. Bailiff considered it from every angle and then, without saying anything to her husband, developed a plan. She might never have put it into effect, as the threat faded and the whole thing slid to the back of her mind, if Tidie had not one day rushed inside from sweeping the veranda and said, "Miss Alicia, come quick. Come see the little girl there."

Mrs. Bailiff felt weak at the news, for she believed the child's mother had finally arrived to create a scene and her first thought was to wonder if her neighbours were at home. She saw instead a tiny girl walking past, her hand held tightly by a bigger one. Neither child even glanced towards the house. Mrs. Bailiff looked uncertainly at Tidie who whispered, "Yes, is she. The little one."

"Child!" Mrs. Bailiff called out loudly. "Yes, you," she said to the bigger girl, who had stopped and turned around at the shout. "Both of you. Come here!"

When both children stepped through the gate, which Tidie opened, and after they had been coaxed onto the veranda – for both showed signs of fear at this new development and at Mrs. Bailiff's voice – Mrs. Bailiff with great care examined the smallest one from head to toe, and seemed satisfied with her sturdy limbs and pleasant face. It bore a distinct look of intelligence, she assured Tidie afterwards – and, of course, of Mr. Bailiff.

"Who is this little child," she asked the bigger girl who was now so cowed she was whimpering.

"Is Miss Mirrie daughter, mam."

"You're her child too?"

"No, mam, is mi anty."

"And who is the child's father?"

"Me doan know mam."

"Come now, you must know," Mrs. Bailiff demanded.

"A doan know… them say is a big man, mam."

Satisfied, Mrs. Bailiff had a last look at the little girl, ordered Tidie to give them bun and cheese, and gave the bigger one some coins, telling her to tell her aunt to come and see her. "Tell her Mrs. Bailiff," she instructed. "Remember that?"

The child's lips trembled with fright, but she repeated the name until she could say it right and, taking the toddler by the hand, promised to do as bid as she rushed them through the gate.

"Tidie," Mrs. Bailiff said expansively, "I am going to take that child. Such a nice little girl. Not a word to Mr. Bailiff, I'm going to bring her here. Give her a good home. That will cure him of his irresponsibility!"

Tidie opened her eyes wide but said nothing.

Ruby ended up in the Bailiff home and, as promised, Mrs. Bailiff said nothing to her husband. That Sunday, she simply propped the little girl up in a high chair pushed to the dinner table before Mr. Bailiff came in, Sunday dinner being the one meal she could count on his being present for.

Mr. Bailiff walked into the dining room, his nose still buried in a newspaper, and took his seat before noticing anything. When he did, he looked at the child and said in his usual jocular manner, "And what have we here?"

"It's your child, Fred," Mrs. Bailiff said, very pleasantly as she unfolded her napkin. "Little Ruby."

Mr. Bailiff, who had passed through the same school of hard knocks as his wife, had also learnt when not to speak. He merely grunted at this news and said nothing more. But Mrs. Bailiff, who was studying him sideways with her eyes fixed firmly on her plate, had the satisfaction of seeing him surreptitiously raise his eyes from time to time to scrutinize the little girl.

Nothing more was ever said and Ruby became a fixture in their household. Over the next few years, news of Ruby's good fortune having travelled among the women patronized by Mr. Bailiff, she was joined by Christopher and Oral, whose mothers brought them and handed them over to Mrs. Bailiff, who accepted them after a wordless examination. Elvis was another matter; he had simply been left on the doorstep, a tiny baby wrapped in a hand-knitted white blanket with a note pinned to it, in large childish letters, *Elvis Baley*. Ordering Tidie to unwrap the bundle and looking as carefully at him as she had scrutinized the other children, Mrs. Bailiff satisfied herself that there could be no doubt about his paternity (though she never confided to anyone how she knew).

Mr. Bailiff received these children with hardly a word, though he increased Mrs. Bailiff's housekeeping allowance each time without being asked, paid for their schooling and provided whatever they needed. He never assumed fatherhood in any other way, nor did he deny it, taking their presence in the house as something perfectly natural, in the same casual manner he took the presence of everyone else around him – including his wife. Mr. Bailiff's experiences had taught him one secret of success: never show surprise at anything.

3

Mrs. Bailiff didn't really care for children. Her own attempts to bear them were based solely on what she thought society expected of her. Tidie was the real caregiver, with other helpers added to the household as needed, to wash and clean and to take Tidie's place temporarily when she herself went off to have her own baby.

Mrs. Bailiff asked no questions about the babyfather, assuming he was someone from Tidie's village, where she had regularly gone once a month for some years till her mother died and she ceased going altogether. The arrangement suited all the children well, for they got to spend a lot of time in the backyard with Tidie and Griff, the gardeners and the other helpers, a yard that kept changing and growing with the passing years, full playground equipment, swimming pool, tennis court added as Mr. Bailiff's rapidly expanding business fortunes swept them all up to bigger and bigger houses.

Mrs. Bailiff's own notions of the requirements of children were somewhat limited to their being seen and not heard, the watchwords of her own mother. Her mother had come from "good family", she always said, though Mrs. Bailiff never came across any of them. By the time she (an only child) had come along, her mother was living by herself in a tenement room and making ends meet by sewing from morning to night. Perhaps her mother's downturn in life, coupled with the heat and allergic reactions to cloth dust, soured her, for she gave little indication of maternal feelings. To keep the growing child from interfering with her clients' precious material by unreeling thread or swallowing pins and needles, Mrs. Bailiff's mother took to tying her to the bed leg for several hours at a time when she was busy, tying her mouth with strips of cloth to shut her up if she persisted in distracting her further with her chatter or her cries.

Mrs. Bailiff, who had little exposure to other people in her childhood, had considered this perfectly normal behaviour at the time. Her mother's harsh treatment taught her two lessons which proved valuable as her life developed: not to speak until absolutely necessary, and to keep her body perfectly still for lengthy periods at a time, the latter a feat which people in social situations with her sometimes found extremely disconcerting. Unfortunately for Mrs. Bailiff, such unnatural bodily stillness served only to agitate the mind and loosen her imagination. Someone with more worldliness or creativity might have put this faculty to good use, but Mrs. Bailiff always felt that one's thoughts should be as tightly reined in as the body. Her childhood thoughts had brought only demons and old higue to ride her, so she desperately tried to curb in her own young charges any flights of fancy, any imaginative spark, anything seeming loose and rattling.

Mrs. Bailiff also knew that cleanliness stood next to godliness, and a healthy mind needed a healthy body, which she maintained with liberal doses of castor oil administered several times a year. The children were well brought up and well maintained, like the houses, the gardens, the cars, but with no notions of warmth or tenderness. Mrs. Bailiff was pleased so long as they appeared clean and healthy, were polite, did well in school, or had their teachers and other adults say nice things about them. With anything else she was unable to cope and either devised devilish punishments in her silent way or threw up her hands and handed them over to Tidie, as she did more and more as both the children and her outside commitments grew.

Elvis was the only real problem child, trying at every opportunity to force his way out of all the straightjacketing. By the time he reached his teens, Mrs. Bailiff gave up on him entirely, praying only that he would grow up quickly, which he did at an alarming rate – and then left home, to her intense satisfaction.

Seeing the children, a group which often included Griff, sitting at the dining table, heads bent over their homework, Mrs. Bailiff always felt immensely gratified that she had managed all this without one word of reproach to her husband. By gathering up and bringing in all his stray children she felt she was striking a telling blow against careless fathers out there (on an island she knew was full of them). She would shame him with her goodness, counter his vile behaviour with the model of family life she would spread before the world, and show him up for the scoundrel he was. *I'm doing this out of the goodness of my heart* was always her first thought as she surveyed the children, and only in her deepest self did a little voice rejoice in the sweet word, "revenge". Her husband would never say, but she could take heart from the knowledge that on this round she had aroused his conscience and beaten him flat.

4

Mrs. Bailiff did not know her husband as well as she thought. Though he could be affable and kind and generous when it suited him, he was also without conscience, especially when it came to matters of substance such as making money, acquiring property, and dealing with women. Far from being shamed by his children's presence as his wife thought, Mr. Bailiff was lionized by his friends and acquaintances, who could not imagine their own wives doing the same thing and, with much slapping on the back, wondered how he got away with it.

In fact, the whole situation was much discussed around town. Everyone was fully aware of the children's paternity, though if Mrs. Bailiff was asked she always did her best to fudge the issue by talking about the "little adopteds". But the menagerie merely added to the Bailiff legend, for the children's growing up and greater visibility coincided with Mr. Bailiff 's rapid rise as real estate dealer (before the introduction of licensing) then property developer, then all-out wheeler-dealer. By the time he got to the pinnacle, everyone had forgotten to ask where Mr. Bailiff had come from or how he had risen so fast, since they would have had to ask that of almost everyone, including themselves.

Mrs. Bailiff could have talked about his origins (from a tenement similar to hers) but not about his business practices which, after the first few years, she had steered clear of. She did not really want to know, and felt her heart give a lurch every time she read or heard of another high-flyer like her husband come crashing down. A new government had recently come to power and the new housing minister was threatening the thorough investigation of real estate operators as part of their campaign platform (though Mr. Bailiff, having wisely donated enormous sums to the party, had kept his name off the list to be investigated up to the time he died).

Rumour even linked Mr. Bailiff to the activities of his son Elvis, though for some this merely added sheen to his legend. Elvis was regarded by a surprising number of people as a modern-day Robin Hood, helping not only in the accumulation but in the redistribution of resources (a popular economic topic of the day). When these particular rumours reached Mrs. Bailiff, she said she could not believe the wickedness of mankind when she knew for a fact her husband had not been in contact with Elvis for years. She repeated this on every possible occasion and especially – with an eye to wide dissemination – at the hairdresser.

5

Mrs. Bailiff was sad to see her husband go, and cried genuine tears the nights after his death. They were used to each other, and he represented the only link to her youth. Yet she also felt a sense of excitement at coming into a lot of property and money on her own. Her husband had always assured her he would leave her well provided for, and it was the one thing he told her that she believed, for he had always been generous in sharing his good fortune with her. So even before the funeral (right after she had sent off the death notice, in fact) she allowed her imagination, which she had managed to suppress all these years, a little flutter. She would do something with herself, she decided, surveying her ample person in the full-length mirror, perhaps rinse out some of the grey, take a little tuck here and there (grabbing folds of flesh).

She was in reasonably good shape for a woman her age, but she had always envied the women she met on the various committees she sat on who kept looking younger and younger every year and made no secret of the new faces and bodies they bought in the USA or Canada, their ability to afford such artifice setting them apart from the common herd. Mrs. Bailiff, despite her no-nonsense self, sometimes thought wistfully that she wished she had the courage to do such things; she knew her husband would have raised no objection to the cost. But she would have been too ashamed to express such desires to him, for it would seem as if she wanted to stay young and attractive to compete with his other women. Now she was free to do anything – buy a new wardrobe, travel, take cruises, sell the house and move into a condo. But when she realized she had no one to share anything with, she felt deflated.

Two of the children were still around. Christopher lived nearby, but was of absolutely no use, being wrapped up totally in his own little world; and though he was developing quite a reputation as an artist, Mrs. Bailiff couldn't see what anyone saw in his paintings, which looked to her exactly like the finger daubs he did as a child except with gross naked women now stuck in (which she attributed to his father's influence). Ruby had recently moved back to the town with her little son after her short-lived marriage and a brief stay in Canada, but she was no fun to be around, having gone from being a happy little girl (for a brief while) to a miserable young woman, and now a sour divorcée whose weight simply kept growing.

Mrs. Bailiff often thought the notion that fat people were supposed to be happy was foolishness. Ruby, who had started to gain weight in her early teens, never showed any signs of happiness. She was secretive, mean, envious, always wanting more, no matter how much you gave her, as if she consisted of nothing more than a hollowness, an insatiable appetite.

None of the children in fact seemed particularly happy, she thought now with surprise, and she wondered why, when they had been given so much. Oral, whose fleet feet had taken him on track scholarships to American universities from which he showed no signs of returning, got in touch only when he wanted funds. Elvis was beyond the pale.

Thinking about it now, Mrs. Bailiff saw the children as nothing but ungrateful, taking for granted all she had done for them out of the goodness of her heart. She felt vindicated in leaving them out of the death announcement, though she noted with surprise that the obituaries paid fulsome attention to them. One paper listed what the writer called their "high achievements in varied fields of endeavour," including Elvis's highly successful security protection services and – amazingly – Ruby's cocktail party catering, which she had given up years before.

6

"No good deed goes unpunished." Mrs. Bailiff was fond of telling herself this phrase after she had discovered it on a little ceramic plaque in a Miami dollar store. She applied it from time to time to the children, but in the early years of their marriage, she thought it applied to her husband. Mrs. Bailiff was convinced it was she who had given her husband his start in life; without her he would have been nothing. She admitted in her most honest moments, she would have been nothing too – but never mind, it was that initial gesture of trust on her part that was the most telling event in their lives together, and she expected forever a corresponding loyalty from him.

The Bailiffs had actually married because Mrs. Bailiff's mother, whom she would in later life think of as a vicious woman, left her a sum of money when she died – substantial for that time, and considering her circumstances. It was for that – to squeeze out every last cent from her working years – that she had treated her child with such cruelty. On her dying bed, Mrs. Bailiff's mother made her swear she would take the money and go to nursing school, for more than anything else she wanted her daughter to have a profession, acquire the status in society she thought she had lost or been denied.

Mrs. Bailiff hated nursing school, and was always grateful to her husband for coming and rescuing her from it. By the time she met him, on the stairs of the boarding house they lived in, he had worked his way up the ladder from sweeping out the office to messenger to salesman for a realtor and auctioneer. He swept her off her feet with the grandeur of his plans and an ambition for self-improvement which matched her own. In those early days the town was surrounded by sugar cane fields on one side and useless scrubland on the other – but he saw, stretching away in those distances, box-like houses, shopping centres, and asphalt parking lots all in neatly laid out rows, just like the pictures of North American suburbs. Mrs. Bailiff never knew where he got his ideas or his drive, for he was born poor and his schooling was minimal, but he had the gift of attracting the patronage of powerful people, whom he impressed with his quick mind, readiness for hard work, ambition and – let it be said – charm. He also had a knack for keeping his ear to the ground, or rather, patronizing the right bars and listening to the knowledgeable clients, and he had a genius for sensing what people's wants were going to be ten and twenty years down the road.

When from time to time he took the young nurse-in-training for an ice cream cone and walks along the seashore, he kept saying all he needed was some capital. "If I could just get my hands on some money," he ended each evening, "… just the piece of land … going for nothing… subdivide… sell… use the money to buy up more land." He would explain his grand schemes to her, using a stick to draw sketches on the ground.

Though she hardly said anything, she was excited by this visionary young man, the first and only boyfriend she had had (for so she thought of him). One day she impulsively said to him,

"How much money do you need?"

"Oh, about ten thousand dollars," he said, naming an impossible sum at that time.

"I have five," she said.

That sealed her fate, once Mr. Bailiff established that she did indeed have money. He was all for borrowing it. "With interest. And papers signed, in a lawyer's office," he said. Then, "If you want to just put it into the business, I'll make you rich."

"I'll give it to you," she said. "And sign all those papers. After we are married."

It was the only time Mr. Bailiff was finessed. But she was not her mother's daughter for nothing. The only thing she remembered of life with her mother was her advice in regard to customers: "Always make sure you collect at least half before you deliver."

At the start, she worked in his office as secretary, receptionist, everything, giving up nursing and making it sound like a big sacrifice. His way of doing business affected her nerves as he sailed close to the wind, with a constant zigzag between bankers, creditors, business associates, government agencies, clients, purchasers, would-be home owners. She didn't have his charm, his assurance, his fluent tongue or his ability to lie. But amazingly – from the perspective of her previously sheltered life – he made a success of it. As soon as they started to make some real money, she gave up the work and he hired a proper secretary, then other staff. Looking back, Mrs. Bailiff realized that her leaving his office, the real centre of his life, had been a parting of sorts, creating a vacuum which had been too promptly filled in every way by Miss Smith. But that, as she was fond of saying, was that.

7

Miss Smith it was who held Mr. Bailiff's growing empire together with an efficient hand. Mrs. Bailiff admired the way Miss Smith had gone from manual typewriter to electric to computer and fax, with such ease – taking every new invention in stride, while remaining in her person so unchanged. Miss Smith looked as if she was born and would die Miss Smith; indeed no one called her by any other name. She lived with her mother – or rather her mother lived with her – in a brand new home in the suburbs (a Bailiff development) driving into town in her rather grand car (changed every few years). Everyone in town (Mrs. Bailiff included) knew Miss Smith provided more than secretarial services to Mr. Bailiff, and the only thing people wondered about was how she managed to do so without losing any of her middle-class old-maidishness in looks and manner.

Mrs. Bailiff's realization of Miss Smith's true position was the first real hurt of her married life. She buried it beneath a sudden interest in the church organ fund and other good works in the town, as if she suddenly felt the need to counter every one of what she construed as her husband's antisocial acts with a positive one of her own. This made her life increasingly harassed, as if she had chained herself to a treadmill. But over time, her feelings towards Miss Smith mellowed. Mrs. Bailiff had to admit that Miss Smith had class; her father had after all been a lawyer, though of slightly tarnished name. Besides – like Tidie – she had also made herself indispensable in the operations of the complex Bailiff household. Miss Smith came to be treated as a family friend, and it was natural that it was she who came and sat with Mrs. Bailiff the nights after her husband's death, sharing the burden of receiving and entertaining those who dropped by, sitting in silent companionship when they were alone, like two widows.

8

Over time, Mrs. Bailiff had worked out a form of coexistence with her husband. She knew he had not married her for love, but in his way he had been good to her. To those women who complained of their husbands' demands and expectations, Mrs. Bailiff had little to say, for her husband left her entirely up to her own devices, only taking her out occasionally to functions when he needed to appear respectable. But though they had come to lead separate lives, Mr. Bailiff – for all his philandering – still liked to have the comforts of his own home and was not above playing the role of the family man when it suited him. Mrs. Bailiff's main virtue was that she never nagged, preserving the intense stillness and silence of her early days. She had reached a stage where so long as she got her share of a comfortable life, she was fine. She had never cared much for the physical side of things. She was attached to Mr. Bailiff as she was to no one else and had long ago decided that while she could exert no control over him outside the home, she would be mistress of what went on inside.

Mrs. Bailiff could have gone to her own grave thinking good thoughts about her late husband, glossing over his weaknesses and exaggerating his good points, for he had been the only man in her life – but in her remaining years she would instead think of him as a cruel, evil, vindictive man, uncaring, without heart. That was after she learned the contents of his will.

9

It wasn't that he had cut her off or deprived her of anything. Indeed, the lawyer and everyone else aware of its contents considered the will more than generous, a tribute from Mr. Bailiff to his wife that assured her he recognized her loyalty, her significance in his life.

There were also some minor bequests. A handsome present to Miss Smith, as expected (in addition to the fine house and furniture, the cars, and everything else she had acquired in his lifetime). To Tidie, a house in a middle-class scheme, which Mrs. Bailiff considered only right and proper after her long and faithful service, though he need not have elevated her to such a desirable residential area. All his remaining property went to Mrs. Bailiff during her lifetime; at her death his estate was to be divided equally among his ten children.

Ten. At first, Mrs. Bailiff thought an error had been made. But no, each child was fully named. *The bastard*, Mrs. Bailiff thought. How could so many of them have slipped through her net? Where had these strays been all this time when she thought she had corralled them all?

So that was what Tidie had been earlier implying. Tidie! Which recalled Mrs. Bailiff to the most powerful shock of all: that the third child Mr. Bailiff named and acknowledged as his own, by birth date a month apart from Christopher, was Jonathan Emmanuel Griffiths, otherwise known as "Griff". On hearing that, Mrs. Bailiff hadn't bothered about the rest of the children. After Oral and Elvis their names meant nothing, they were merely insects crawling out of the woodwork everywhere, nibbling at the very foundations of her house. Tidie's treachery was unbearable. The nerve of the woman, looking so pleased when she was summoned by the lawyer to be told she had been left a house by the Mister. Displaying not a shred of shame.

Mrs. Bailiff was so drained by the revelations that she didn't bother to deal with Tidie, expecting her to clear out by the next day anyway, rushing to move into her very own house. But much to her surprise, Tidie appeared the next morning as usual, acting as if nothing had happened, except she couldn't wipe the smile from her face.

"Imagine, Miss Alicia," she said, serving Mrs. Bailiff her usual breakfast. She took up her standard pose when she had important news to impart, her feet braced in her slippers and arms folded across her chest at the dining room door. "Imagine," she said dreamily (like the smiles, a new state for her), "Me is the only babymother the Mister name in him Will! Me one him give house to. The Mister don't even fenny on the rest of them." And with that she burst into a raucous laugh. "Keh-keh-keh." It could be heard echoing loudly behind her as she moved towards the kitchen.

Mrs. Bailiff half rose from her chair, intending to order Tidie from the premises once and for all. But she was overcome with a tiredness that was new to her and sat down again, feeling – for the first time in her life – defeated. Amazingly, after that outburst, Tidie fell back into her normal self. She was never heard cackling with laughter again, though from time to time she forgot to wipe the smile from her face in Mrs. Bailiff's presence.

One day, when Mrs. Bailiff could finally bring herself to speak about the matter uppermost in her mind, she said through clenched teeth, "Tidie, I don't understand you. How come in all these years you could never find it in your heart to tell me Griff's father was the Mister? How you could be so secretive and bad-minded? Don't you think I had a right to know?"

"But Miss," Tidie protested earnestly. "How I could faas

enough to tell you such a thing? After you never ask?"

Mrs. Bailiff silently closed her eyes and lifted her thoughts to Heaven.

10

So Mr. Bailiff spoiled his wife's remaining years, though those who had known him wondered how his behaviour in death could weigh more on her mind than his actions in life. "It takes all sorts," people muttered when they heard Mrs. Bailiff had gone into a decline and taken to her fine mahogany four-poster bed. Those who assumed it was from grief were very wrong. Mrs. Bailiff was stewing in her own anger, steeping herself in acid that in time would dry up the heart she was so proud of, a heart from which such goodness once flowed. She had seen her life with Mr. Bailiff as something of a duel, with herself constantly trying to counteract his vilest misdeeds, but he had managed to go to his grave as winner of the most crucial duel of all. How could she have been so wrong? Mrs. Bailiff felt limp, so foolish, such a failure, like Aeolus, from whom all the winds of the world escaped just when he was congratulating himself for having everything knotted up and firmly under control.

Just a few years earlier, Mrs. Bailiff's withdrawal from the life of the town would have been felt as keenly as that of her husband's. She was the most formidable of the formidable ranks of older women with time on their hands, who organized everything they considered wholesome. Libraries and crèches, soup kitchens, hospital Christmas treats, books for prisoners, clothing for the poor, animal hospitals, fluoride in the drinking water – nothing was beyond them. However, in Mrs. Bailiff's later years, people like her were being swept away like dried sea-almond leaves before the winds or, perhaps more accurately, by the new brooms provided to street cleaners by a new government embarked on sweeping change. The people were to take their destiny into their own hands, they were told; they no longer needed the likes of Mrs. Bailiff to organize them. So Mrs. Bailiff, whose presence alone could have made the very trees tremble, vanished like so many others before the mantra of self-reliance.

Those who did cross her threshold could not help but notice an astringent smell pervading the house. The smell was nothing new, for Mrs. Bailiff had always required not just ordinary cleanliness that came from soap and store-bought cleansers, but the assurance from things that she knew could really scour: Seville orange for the wooden floors, cut limes for the sinks and counter tops, bath cleaning finished with vinegar in the water, tamarind drink and acid lemonades for the children, Seville orange and other bitter marmalades and seeded grapefruits for the breakfast table, Bay Rum saturating the head and body for every imagined ailment, lime cologne as freshener when leaving the house.

When Mr. Bailiff was alive, his sweetness counteracted the acidity. Even though his presence was so minimal – he came home only to shower and dress, except for Sunday when he spent part of the day with the family – his scent, which was compounded of expensive soaps, shaving creams, aftershaves, colognes, always lingered, clung to every nook and cranny of the house, as if mocking the healthy reputation of citric acids. Mr. Bailiff was in every sense of the phrase a "sweet man". With him gone forever, astringency was in the ascendant – though sometimes Mrs. Bailiff found herself ambushed in her sleep by a sweet scent, and she would totter out of bed in the middle of the night to rub cut lime over a surface or object, unaware that she was already protected by the acid that had crept into her heart.

Despite her otherwise admirable control, she couldn't help this acid occasionally gushing forth in little bursts, directed at the only other person now present in the house.

"Why don't you just go," she screamed one day at Tidie, who was in the room dusting. She said this for no reason at all. "Don't you get what you want already? Don't you have your own house?"

Tidie gave no indication of surprise. As she lightly slapped the feather duster against the bed post, she answered in her serviceable matter-of-fact tone, "I not going to go and leave you, Miss

Alicia. How me could do that?" Mrs. Bailiff was suddenly suffused with a warm glow, thinking the world was not a bad place
after all when such loyalty prevailed. Tidie continued, pausing
with duster in hand and looking straight at her mistress with
innocent eyes: "Why me should go and me have job? What me
going to sit down and do? Me rent out the house while me living
here so me can have something put by for mi old age, for is so
Lawyer tell me fe do. Me not leaving you, Miss Alicia."

In the pause, Mrs. Bailiff felt so suffused by Tidie's kindness
that a smile started to appear on her face, the first since the reading
of the will – only to be wiped off instantly by Tidie's next words,
spoken in the same tone as everything else.

"Me not leaving till you die. And Griff get him inheritance."
With that she went back to dusting.

Mrs. Bailiff felt the bile rise up in her. She wondered again, as
she had done many times since Mr. Bailiff's death, whether Tidie
was the simple innocent she had always imagined or the vilest
schemer on earth.

Nevertheless, it was Tidie's comment that gave Mrs. Bailiff a
different take on things – a second wind, so to speak, that enabled
her to throw off her lethargy and get set for a new engagement
with life. No, she would never become a community activist, as
paid people who did the unpaid voluntary work she once did were
now called. She had no more interest in helping others. She
remained steadfastly at home, still kept invasion at bay with
vinegar and limes. But now she summoned to her side a new host
of people never before seen crossing her threshold, but soon
beating a path. Hairdresser, interior decorator, masseuse, the girl
who did nails, the lady who did faces, and experts on mud baths,
colonic irrigation, papaya face peels, yoga, tai chi, aromatherapy,
body wraps, feng shui, to name a few. She put herself under the
care of a holistic practitioner and paid for the flight to her bedside
of a woman whom the papers announced was schooled in
iridology. She took to reading the papers and magazines again,
watching television, and even having movies brought in to watch
on the video, reverting to the partiality in her youth for old-style

shoot-em-up Westerns. She got a large satellite dish installed so she could keep up with the very latest in medical breakthroughs, wonder drugs and other secrets of longevity. She summoned to her house and paid handsomely anyone who could bring her a promise of good health and renewed vitality.

This had nothing to do with the revitalization she had wished for when Mr. Bailiff was still alive. All of this activity was fuelled by only one thought. *The bastards! Just let them wait!* Mrs. Bailiff had decided she would dry up the juices of her heart to preserve it and, with the help of money and science, seduce the rest of her body to youthful suppleness, use up the children's inheritance like rejuvenation cream. She intended to live on and on and on.

LOLLIPOP

Miss Katie and the vacuum cleaner are engaged in their usual struggle. They are evenly matched in size; Katie is small for her age and the vacuum cleaner is a huge old monster, heavy and own-way. Katie is only just getting used to electricity and is scared every time she has to plug anything in. When she turns the beast on, it roars and bucks out of control. Sometimes it reduces Katie to tears. But she doesn't give up. She spends a lot of time washing up and cleaning and scouring and tidying. She wants her mother to know she has a useful daughter, one who knows how to do things and not one come to suck her blood, as she says every time she is vexed.

★

Miss Katie learned usefulness from her grandmother. Gran is the one who stuck the "Miss" onto her name from the time Katie was small-small. If Miss Katie wasn't there to look after the two little ones, Gran always said, how she could leave them alone in the yard and go to her day's work, and where would they be then? When Gran said such a thing, Katie's spirits lifted and she didn't feel so tired running after the little ones all day or be vexed at missing school again.

Her mother doesn't call her Miss Katie; she doesn't know that name, she left for Canada before Katie became useful to Gran. She calls her "Katherine" which is her rightful name. It is in the brand new passport that brought her to Toronto and the name they will use when she goes to school. She is getting used to the name; "Katherine" is making her feel big and grown up and she's glad she isn't answering to "Miss Katie" anymore and can put that country-bumpkin self behind her. Now that she is here, in the big city of Toronto, what a joke it would be for people to hear her called that. Especially for Kirton, who is the only person she knows in Toronto – other than Kirton's friend, Krishna.

She saw Kirton the very first day she stepped onto the balcony by herself, saw him right there on his beside-hers balcony, as close as if he could reach over and touch her. What if she had answered "Miss Katie" when he asked her for her name? She would never live it down. Especially since she found out that she and Kirton would be going to the same school. Worse, that they would be in the same grade, though how that was possible Katie didn't know, for Kirton was twice her size whether she looked him up or looked him across. No wonder as he never stopped eating. Food in one hand, the other attached to some gadget which he called "Play-Station" and which he was forever clicking. Most of the time Kirton was on the balcony playing by himself, but sometimes Krishna was there, too. Krishna lived in the apartment across the hall and would also be in her class. She was relieved that he was closer to her in size and quieter. He smiled a lot and let Kirton do the talking.

★

When Katie is done tidying and cleaning, she throws all the waste in the plastic bag in the pail in the kitchen and expertly twists the mouth to tie it tight. Then she takes a clean white plastic bag and puts it inside the pail and smooths it over the edge. Miss Katie is neat and precise in everything she does, for that is how Gran is – in her home and at her work. Katie knows because every now and then, when her employers were away, she took Katie to work with her in their big house, so she would know how to do things properly, Gran said. Katie is pleased that though they had none of these things at Gran's house, she had come to Canada knowing how to clean the bath and scour the toilet, use the vacuum and the floor polisher and the washing machine. Katie knows how to light

a gas stove too, v-e-r-y c-a-r-e-f-u-l-l-y or it will go "BOOM,"
Gran warned. But though her mother's stove is electric, it's the
one thing she is not allowed to touch. Never mind she told her
mother she could cook.

"Cook mi backfoot! You mean boil yam and dumpling and
green banana? Well, we don't eat them things up here. Just don't
touch the stove, you hear me? I don't want you burn down the
place. A-oh."

So Katie didn't touch the stove, though she didn't know what
made her mother say these things in such a cross voice – as if Katie
would really do a thing like that. Katie would have preferred to
cook something nice rather than eat what her mother brought
home in the evenings.

Until she came to Toronto, Katie only knew food that came
out of the ground or off a tree, with a little meat or a bit of chicken
or saltfish once a week. At school she always had a patty and coco
bread for lunch and a box of chocolate milk. Her schoolmates
complained about the canteen fare and always talked about eating
Fast Food when they went to town with their parents. Katie was
envious of their air of sophistication when they said this, though
she never let on. When Gran took her to town to get her passport
and her papers, she passed several golden arches and the fried
chicken places and recognized them instantly. From the bus she
looked longingly at how lit up inside these places were, how
inviting they seemed, wondering what "Fast Food" really meant,
but Gran moved too fast for them to stop and find out. Now she
wonders if what her mother brings home is Fast Food. She thinks
of it as "box food" for even when heated up it tastes like cardboard.
Her mother always brings enough food so Katie can have the
leftovers for lunch the next day and has shown her how to "zap"
the food in the microwave, but Katie is too afraid to try, she just
isn't a zapper. She isn't used to eating cold food from the fridge
either. Gran didn't have a fridge but she always said eating cold
food straight out of the fridge makes you sick. That's why the lady
she worked for couldn't keep any good health, Gran said, always
just opening the fridge door and picking at things.

★

Katie puts away the vacuum cleaner and looks around the tiny apartment, pleased with her handiwork. She looks at the television in anticipation. Her mother says she can watch when she finishes all the work. Katie is so obedient she wouldn't dream of taking a break and watching before she was done. Now there is only one thing left to do, the hardest thing.

She hangs the apartment key around her neck and picks up the plastic bag with the garbage. Making sure the door is locked behind her, she sets off down six flights to the garbage bins at the back of the building. She hates going down the stairs by herself; the stairwell is dirty and dimly lit and smelly. But she is even more scared of getting into the creaky old elevator by herself.

Of late, she's forgotten how she hates the stairwell. The beads in her braids go clickety-clack as she moves and she goes faster and faster down the stairs and flashes her hair to speed up the rhythm. The beaded braids are a signal that her mother loves her after all, that Katie is not a bloodsucking vampire. Despite complaining about how much it would cost, her mother had taken her to her friend Vinnie on Eglinton to have her hair done, claiming that she couldn't be seen with a child whose hair was so picky-picky and countryish and why Katherine's grandmother couldn't have had her hair styled before sending her over. After all the money she send. And how she had let Katherine get so skinny, pure skin and bones. Look nuh, Vinnie. Lifting up Katie's T-shirt to show her ribs. All this as Vinnie labours over Katie's hair. And how much money she there sending every month, what she doing with it, and how much it cost to bring Katherine over, the lawyer alone.

Katie has heard this many times before, which is why her mother is holding down two jobs and tired on weekends, so has no time to take Katie anywhere.

Her mother talking about sending money every month made Katie pause, for she remembers Gran complaining all the while that Lisa had forgotten she left three children behind when she went about her business and must be air she expect me to feed them on. Every month she made Katie write a letter to her mother reminding her to send money. Her mother hardly ever wrote back, though Katie had strict instructions to stop at the post office every day on the way home from school and ask if there were letters for Gran. Once in a blue moon Katie's mother dropped them a few brief lines and sent them something. So if she sent money every month, where did it go?

★

Katie wonders how Gran is managing without her, for Gran can't read and she relied on Katie to handle anything that required reading and writing from when Katie was small-small. If the letter came from Government even if it was typed Katie couldn't make out a lot of the words, try as she might, or they had no meaning – NOT-WITHSTANDING – although Gran said it was okay. She was ashamed Gran sometimes had to take the letter to Miss Lue at the shop and ask her to tell her what it said. Gran preferred to ask Miss Lue than one of the neighbours, because she said Miss Lue knew how to keep her mouth shut which is more than black people knew.

There was this one time, after Gran came out of the hospital and her sister Aunt Gwen was packing up to go back home, for Gran had to call her urgent urgent to come and look after the children. "It is time that wutless daughter of mine take on her responsibility," Gran told Aunt Gwen, with one hand to her back as if she needed help to straighten up. "Ah can't do it anymore. Ah don't know why she don't send for the children. Look how long she promise. From Katie just gone four until now, look Katie turn big girl almost ready to take Common Entrance. Who is going to pay to keep her in high school? Where all the man them gone to that she said was going to support them? You see any father about? Gwen, I done with it. Finish, finish, finish!" And Gran, standing straight, slapped her palms together several times to signify how done she was. "Ah going to write that girl and give her a piece of my mind. If she don't hear me, is Government going have to take them over! A-oh."

Katie jerked her head back from the doorway where she was listening. As if Gran had given her a stinging blow. Government to take them over? She meant the three of them? Like those bad children that live in the Home down the road? After she and her little brothers never do anything bad? How Gran could threaten them so? Katie couldn't ask Gran if she would really do that, for she wasn't supposed to be listening to big people talk. But the possibility of something so monstrous grew and grew inside her the way a big fat pumpkin grew and grew, until she could barely breathe. It made her tired even to play hopscotch.

But it wasn't long before she got her feelings ease. As soon as Gran was up to it, she walked slowly down to the shop and asked Miss Lue to write the letter which she brought home and gave to Katie to take to the post office, all sealed and stamped. "Now. Directly, Miss Katie," she ordered. "It can't wait till tomorrow." The letter was like a bomb in Katie's hand and she ran all the way; she didn't know what piece of her mind Gran had put inside. Something like the gas that would go BOOM if mishandled, which is probably why she didn't want Katie to write this letter. Or keep it in the house till Katie could drop it off on her way to school next day. It was something only big people could handle.

Maybe a letter written by a big person was better than one written by a little one, especially when her big square letters barely joined up while Miss Lue's handwriting on the envelope swooped and swirled as if the ink just danced out of the pen. Once that letter danced over to her mother in Toronto and that piece of mind Gran put inside said BOOM, her mother got off her You-Know-What and began to take out Katie's papers. She promised Gran she would send for Katie first and the boys later. She couldn't manage all of them at once. So said Gran, waving around the letter that Katie had just read aloud to her, repeating everything back as if it was news. Then she folded it up and put it in the old biscuit tin, where she kept important matters, pushing the tin back under the bed on which they all slept and muttered, "Well, you'd better mean it this time, my girl."

Katie noticed that Gran's face was grim. Gran's face was grim all the time now as if she was always in pain. Sometimes without asking, she made Gran lemonade and brought it to her and once she gave her the whole of a chocolate bar Miss Lue had given her, pretending that she had already eaten hers. Gran ate it, slowly, all by herself; such a thing had never happened before in her life, Gran said, having a whole chocolate bar she didn't have to share with pikni. Katie got so much enjoyment watching Gran eat that chocolate that she didn't miss not having any.

★

In Toronto not a soul could say that Katie was short of chocolates and sweeties, for her mother liked to eat them herself; the big jar on the kitchen counter was always full. At first Katie gorged herself, especially when her mother went out and left her alone at night. But she cut back when she thought about getting as big as Kirton – that is what eating did to you they said on television. Whenever she knew she had had enough, she would hear Gran's voice saying, "Greedy choke puppy" and "When you go to that big country, Miss Katie, it have everything there. Everything a person could want in the whole wide world. But don't get big-eye. Don't turn wanti-wanti. Promise. You hold strain and think of them poor little ones back here that don't have nothing. Eat for one, lest you turn into two."

Gran ate for one and she was big as two or three. And Katie's mother ate sweets and chocolates all the time, huge quantities of food when she came home from work, yet she stayed slender as bamboo. Maybe Gran's warning applied to Kirton. Kirton's parents were just like him, only twice his size. Kirton's mother was home all day with the television going full blast, and every now and then she would yell from inside for Kirton and Kirton would disappear for a moment or two, or she would come out as far as the doorway to hand him a plate with something. Kirton's father was

big, too, the one time Katie passed him and Kirton in the corridor.
The only time Kirton went out was when his father came on
weekends and took him. Katie wondered if having a mother that
was home all day was better than a mother who was never at home.

★

Not that Katie's mother wants anyone to know she leaves Katie
alone. She made Katie swear she won't talk to anyone in the
building and she won't answer the door, ever, if anyone knocks.
Her mother said Government would come and take Katie away
and put her mother in jail if they found out, for Katie was
underage.

Katie asked why and Katie's mother said that's how Government up here stay. Katie told her mother that Gran said one time
she was going to hand Katie and her brothers over to Government
and Katie's mother said, "Cho, that not nothing. Government
there is a joke. You think them care bout people pikni? Is here you
must come if you want to know how Government can faas in yu
business. Childrens Services. Poppyshow! Once them come
after you, girl, is dog nyam your supper."

Katie feels bad that her mother has to work so hard. She works
in a hotel in the day but Katie isn't sure what kind of work she does
at night. It is work she has to dress up for though, in high heels
and everything, or dress down, for she doesn't put much on
though she always throws on a jacket before she goes out. Katie
likes to watch her mother getting ready, the way she put on her
makeup and fiddles with her braids, sometimes putting them up,
sometimes leaving them down. Katie is dying to grow tall and
beautiful like her mother.

On Sundays her mother doesn't work. They go to the laundro-
mat and afterwards to a restaurant nearby for lunch. Katie loves
to sit at a table or best of all a booth so it's just the two of them in
the whole world and eat real food. Sometimes her mother talks
without looking at Katie, like she's looking at nothing at all.

"It's not that I don't love my children you know. I'm really trying. But people down there don't know how hard life is up here. I never out of debt yet, for the first thing I had to pay off was my fare. Clothes for winter. Somewhere to live. You think a person can live on minimum wage? Can't keep body and soul together."

Sometimes she talks directly to Katie as if she is a big person. "I was too young to have children. I was just a pikni meself, never know a thing about life. Don't bother start ya, Katherine. Make sure you get education first."

She looks fully at Katie then, as if only just realizing who she is, gives a sad smile and reaches out to touch Katie's cheek.

"Katherine, I don't want you to think I don't love you. I'm glad you come."

By the time the food arrives, Katie feels as if she has already feasted.

★

Katie's mother said the next weekend she would take Katie to buy everything she needed for school. So now Katie had something to announce on the balcony to put that big-head boy Kirton in his place for always boasting about all the places his father had taken him.

But when Katie announced, "My mother is taking me to Honest Ed to buy my school things this Saturday," Kirton laughed.

"Honest Ed! You crazy! Zellers in the only place to buy stuff. You know what my mother gets with her Zed points?"

"My mother buys everything at Costco. That is the best," Krishna put in. This started the boys on some heated argument about what was the best of everything. Katie didn't know what they were talking about. When Kirton said if she turned up at school looking uncool the children would laugh at her, Katie screwed up her face and started crying. It was too much, she blubbered. She hadn't set foot in their school yet and everything she did was wrong!

Kirton paused with a slice of pizza halfway to his mouth.

"Hush Katherine," Krishna said, "Kirton is only joking." He elbowed Kirton as he said this.

"Ah Katherine," Kirton said in his lazy voice, "I didn't know you were a crybaby."

"I'm not."

"Don't worry. Nobody will trouble you at school. I'll look out for you." Kirton said this in a nicer voice; then, as if that took care of everything, he shoved the food into his mouth.

"Me too," said Krishna. "If anybody trouble you Katherine, just let them come... let them come..." Skinny Krishna balled up his fists and danced like a boxer when he said this, which made Katie laugh. She dried her eyes, pleased at this pledge of support, though deep down she wasn't sure if Kirton was the kind of person who would do her much good at school.

★

Even more than the stairs, Katie hates opening the back door and going into the enclosed concrete yard where the big garbage bins are located. Big and smelly and usually overflowing. But what she really hates is The Man. She knows he looks after the place; her mother told her so one time they passed him mopping the entranceway as they were going out. Her mother said "Hey Don," and he leaned against the mop and said hello and smiled. He has an apartment in the basement and sometimes it is just Katie's luck that he comes out as she reaches up on tiptoe to throw her garbage in the bin.

The first time he said "Hello Katherine," she nearly died of fright as she hadn't seen him in the shadow of the building, smoking a cigarette.

The man is pleasant to her and always smiling so she doesn't know why he makes her feel shivery – like the time a boy at school threw a lizard on her. The lizard landed on her back and she screamed and spun around but the lizard held on tighter and tighter and her blood ran cold. Maybe because the man is what

Gran would call frennie-frennie – trying too hard to be a friend. And he is too faas, for he seems to know everything. He knows Katie's name and that Lisa is Katie's mother. He knows where she comes from. He knows where she will be going to school and what grade she'll be in.

And today, he makes Katie's heart fall clear to her foot-bottom because he knows that her mother leaves Katie alone! What he says is, "Don't worry, kiddo. If anything happens when you are up there alone, just give ol' Dan a call and I'll come quicker than Holy Moses. Your Ma has my number posted right by the phone."

Katie's heart jumps. How does he know what is by their phone? He speaks Canadian in a funny kind of way and Katie doesn't understand half of what he says. More than anything, she doesn't believe his smile. She is too polite to run away while he is speaking and too scared to speak herself though her heart is hammering: tell him no, tell him your mother never leaves you alone. But the words won't come and Katie is stuck, between the smelly overflowing garbage bins and the man who stands between her and the door.

Suddenly he takes a step closer to her and says, "Don't be so shy, Kiddo. I'm your friend. Here," and he extends his hand. Katie automatically shuts her eyes and shrinks away. When nothing happens, she opens them to see that the man is holding out a lollipop. She shakes her head. No she doesn't want it, but he comes real close and holds the lollipop up to her face and says quiet-quiet, "Go on, take it Katherine. I got it specially for you." And when Katie still doesn't move, he whispers, still smiling, "Don't worry, I'm not going to tell anyone that your Ma leaves you alone up there."

Katie feels trapped, she doesn't want the man's offering, but she doesn't want to offend. In one quick move, she reaches out and grabs the lollipop and dances around him and races for the door. She runs up the stairs so fast she has to stop several times to catch her breath, afraid to look behind her. Once inside the apartment she slams the door and leans against it and takes great gulps of air. It is only when she comes back to her rightful self, sitting on the sofa, that Katie realizes that she is still holding the lollipop. She rushes to the kitchen and flings it into the garbage bin the way she flung the lizard away. It lies on top of the white plastic bag that hasn't been pushed all the way down.

Katie goes back to the couch and doesn't bother to switch on the television, or turn on a light. She sits, hugging herself, waiting for her mother to come home so she can tell her that someone knows, the man knows, and she never wants to put out the garbage again. Katie jumps at every little sound, not trusting the lock to hold anyone who wants to burst the door down.

She must have fallen asleep, but as soon as her mother comes through the door she jumps up at once, crying, "Mama —"

Her mother doesn't pause as she sweeps into the kitchen, where she leaves a bag on the counter, and dashes for the bedroom, kicking off her shoes as she runs. "Not now Katherine, I'm late," she calls out. "Damn and blast ttc. And I don't eat a thing from morning. Share out the food for me, nuh."

Katie doesn't move. Her eyes fill with tears. Her mother comes back out barefoot in bra and panty.

"Girl, what's wrong with you, you deaf?" she cries, and moves like lightning into the kitchen, opening cupboard doors, pulling down plates, and rattling the cutlery drawer. The activity ceases and Katie hears her mother say, in a different, quiet tone, "Katherine, what is this?"

Katie looks up to see her mother standing in the kitchen door holding up the lollipop that she'd thrown in the garbage. She wets her lips for she wants to tell her about the man and how he scares her, but nothing comes out.

"I ask you a question, Miss. Answer me."

Katie stays silent even though she can feel her mother working herself into a rage, the air already crackling.

"A-oh, so now you throwing away food, eh? We have so much that we can afford to just throw things in the garbage. Oh yes, money grows on trees and the streets of Canada are paved with gold."

This voice is the one Katie dreads the most, for it is high and criss.

"You know what, Miss, I am going to confiscate this; no more sweets for a week." Her mother indicates the jar of sweets.

Katie notices that the lollipop her mother has placed on the counter is identical to the ones in the jar. She wants to explain but no words come. Her mother is still talking.

"Here," she says, holding out the lollipop. "Go on, take it."

Katie doesn't move. Her mother grabs her hand and slaps the lollipop into her palm and closes her fingers over it.

"That's your dinner tonight. You are going to stand right here and eat that lollipop till it finish. You hear me? Stand here." And she pulls Katie to a spot in the kitchen. "Start now. Waste not, want not. I don't know what your Grannie teach you, but I not going to let you bring any bad habit into this house."

Her mother looks steadily at her until Katie rouses herself. Taking hold of the stick, she peels the paper off the lollipop. The cellophane crackles loudly.

"Go on."

Katie puts the sweet in her mouth, trying not to gag.

"Right. I am going to get ready so don't try no foolishness. When I come back I want to see that you suck that lollipop till it finish, finish." And just as Gran would have done, her mother slaps her palms together several times to signal doneness, before dashing into the bathroom and slamming the door.

Katie stands there, hands straight by her side, with the lollipop in her mouth. She feels herself folding in like a shamey-weed that's been stepped on. She tries to think of something and all that comes to mind is how Kirton is such a don't-care boy. How at first he frightened her with his questions, questions raining down so much Katie was afraid to go out on the balcony. But it was the only place to see a bit of the sky, get some fresh air and, once she got used to it, look right down onto the street full of cars and people. Every time she got tired of staying inside because she was afraid of Kirton, she would tell herself it was her mother's balcony and she would go out there as she liked and ignore the facety white boy. But Kirton was impossible to ignore. He just had to catch the littlest glimpse of a person standing in the doorway before he started talking. Katie is thinking she could harden her heart like Kirton and ignore every little thing. Be a don't-care girl. O yes, and it would serve her mother right. When the Government come and take me away and send me back to mi Gran. What she going to do then?

She throws a cut-eye in her mother's direction and fiercely struggles with the tears that are threatening. Already the lollipop filling her mouth is tasting like box food. No sweetness at all.

BOXED-IN

1

Whenever his name was recalled, people said it was a shame that Mr. Everett never lived to make the move to Town with the rest of them; he would have enjoyed it so, especially watching television, which was now the newest of the new things that had come their way.

Shortly before the move, they found him sitting bolt upright in his chair on the veranda, stiff and cold, staring straight ahead with shocked, wide-open eyes. He was the last person to be buried in the graveyard, and the last dead for whom they danced Dinki Mini, for such things were to have no place in Town. At the graveside, everyone made sure to stand with his or her back to the grave and throw a clump of the fresh earth between their legs to prevent his duppy from following them home. They planted gungo peas to tie him to the grave, and Mrs. Everett took to wearing her specially made navy-blue undergarments inside out. No one could have too much protection, the other widows cautioned her. She was a great deal younger than Mr. Everett, too young to spend the rest of her life alone; the duppy could spoil her for other men.

Although Mr. Everett's death was sudden, it was not unexpected. In the last few weeks of his life, he had already begun to show signs of wanting to move on to another sphere; he rejected all the things that had formerly engaged him. He vanished by degrees, right before their eyes, becoming thin and skeletal from his refusal of food, then dirty, smelly, bearded, and wild-haired from neglecting himself. He responded to none of their efforts to help him. It was as if he had allowed Death to come and claim him long before breath left his body.

Still, up to the end, nobody gave up on him.

"As soon as you move to town, buy a television. You will see how that will cheer him up," their neighbour Mr. Bailey told Mrs. Everett when she confided, for the umpteenth time, her fears concerning her husband's condition.

Had it been any other time, there would have been far more concern about Mr. Everett. Indeed, his sudden failing would have been regarded with suspicion, and steps taken immediately to find out the cause and counteract it. But it happened just as everyone was getting ready for the final move, to surrender the familiar red clay earth surrounding their mountain homes to the Canadian mining company, which had bought every hill and gully in sight. There was an air of bustle and anticipation as one family after another packed up to leave. For months, everyone had been caught up in the excitement of moving. Everyone except Mr. Everett.

He had taken to spending his time sitting on his front veranda, slumped in his wooden chair with his feet up on the veranda railings, seemingly unaware of everything, even the little girls who called out greetings as they passed. He, who normally had such an appetite for life, now wanted nothing. He ignored everyone, even Mr. Bailey, not just neighbour but lifelong friend.

It got so bad that Bailey took to loudly proclaiming that he would not set foot inside Mr. Everett's yard again, not even when they moved to Town, where they had bought houses side by side in a brand new development. Bailey said it on several occasions, adding each time one of his favourite sayings, such as "Independent Jankro fly high", "One person cannot quarrel", "Spread yu bed hard and you lie down on it" or – his favourite – "Man never know the value of water till the spring run dry." He moved closer and closer to the croton hedge between their houses and spoke more loudly each time; he was a bit of a joker. He did this expecting Mr. Everett to come to his senses and call out a reply in the same vein. Then, as he was accustomed to do in the cool of the evening, he could stroll over for a game of draughts, a tot of rum, and some singing. But no call came. Mr. Everett – prosperous citizen, village lawyer, church deacon, and king of their little world in the mountains – had suddenly and unaccountably locked everyone out.

They had no way of knowing that Mr. Everett was in fact desperately trying to lock everything in, to make his thoughts as secure inside his head as if he had placed them in a strong box. For he had suddenly seen with his own eyes what snares were out there waiting to entangle, to capture, and to exhibit one's secret life to the world.

2

Mr. Everett's withdrawal could be dated precisely to the day Bailey first introduced him to a television set – the very box Bailey was now instructing Mrs. Everett to purchase, to revive her husband's flagging spirits. Mr. Everett first saw the object of his demise in the new electrical store on the main street of the town, sitting in the middle of the big plate-glass window. The box was made of a hard shiny substance that was obviously strong enough to keep hostage and withstand the stirrings of the powerful forces it had captured inside of it. As those knowledgeable would expect, it was painted black so the unearthly blue light which was emitted only through its glasslike front – the kind of light Mr. Everett associated with powerful manifestations – could not otherwise escape.

Fortunately he first viewed it around 10 a.m., in bright sunlight when no spirits are abroad, so he was at first more curious than afraid, approaching it as he did from an oblique angle. But when Mr. Everett pushed past the idlers who were constantly congregated outside the store window and walked right up to stare the box fully in its face, he got such a gut-wrenching fright that a ghost, familiar of his world, would have been far less disturbing. Inside the box, there were people! Moving, waving their hands, opening their mouths as if talking, occupying a world just like that on Earth.

While all newcomers to the box spent their time speculating on how television worked, Mr. Everett did not get that far. He was immediately struck by its implications and it rooted him to the spot. It was the greatest Science he had ever seen. Someone had invented a box that could not only reduce people and their world to doll size, but get inside their houses, capture their images as they crossed the street or got on a bus, ran across a field or ate their food, display to every idle passer-by what they were doing in the privacy of their homes. He even witnessed two people kissing!

Mr. Everett had no idea who these captives were. But they seemed totally unaware that strangers were watching their every move. Here was this woman in her dining room laying a table. Mr. Everett, despite himself, was just getting used to her – admiring her straight body in that neat dress, her cute little apron, her pageboy hairdo, her high heels in the kitchen – when suddenly a man entered through the door. The man was shouting and waving his hands, he was angry. Mr. Everett wanted to shout a warning to the woman, but pulled himself up short, glad he had not done so; these were rich white people, the type who would never let the likes of him into their fancy homes.

For some unaccountable reason, the scene was at that point interrupted by a smiling man standing in front of a brand new car to which he pointed, his mouth opening and closing as he walked around it, as if inviting someone standing out of sight to admire its features.

As Mr. Everett watched, he began to feel less and less anxious, began to enjoy the antics. The man and the car disappeared, to be replaced by a man and woman all dressed up and dancing with long, gliding steps. He could see now this was a world of action, of people coming and going at a speed that was dizzying, scenes forever changing. He could see the people's lips were moving, and when he followed Bailey into the store he realized the boxes – there he saw several more – had also captured sound.

After that introduction, he went back more than once to view the people inside the box in the store window. He became more and more convinced that they were spirits, for they were all as white as chalk. In the nether world, all became pale and ethereal, each indistinguishable from the other; it was a world in which people were remarked not by appearance but by behaviour. This made him less anxious about the box. If its activities were centred not in this life, but in the world of spirits, a parallel universe, it was something he could understand. One of Mr. Everett's closely guarded secrets was that he dabbled in the spirit world himself – not that he would have used the word "dabbled" for something he regarded with such seriousness. He began to think it might be possible to learn a thing or two from the box, and invented excuses for going more frequently to Town – something he had avoided in the past – to watch the flickering world of ghosts in the shop window.

One day, he got a rude awakening when an unmistakably black face appeared in the box, one he knew could be no spirit. He rushed inside the store to hear what it was saying, and his knees almost buckled under him. The handsome young black man was singing the very songs Mr. Everett and the rest of the villagers were accustomed to singing at every roof raising or digging-match – when those things still happened. How had they got hold of their songs? "A chi chi Bud, O," the young man sang in a honey-like baritone. "Some a dem a holla, some a bawl." Mr. Everett's discomfiture was complete when the man broke into "Day O. Day da light and me want to go home," just like the banana loaders down on the coast. It was the very song he and Bailey had been given to singing together, in fun, so many evenings before the box had parted them – as it had, though Bailey didn't know it.

The power of the box, Mr. Everett now knew, was complete. It was everywhere. It was here. He was glad Bailey had not come to Town with him, for this time he would not have been able to keep his thoughts to himself. He was so frightened he had to stop at the nearest rum bar for a few stiff whites before making his way home. Power was something Mr. Everett understood, having spent a great part of his life acquiring and using it. In his world, power had a source and a price. He had no idea of the source of this new power and shuddered at the thought of what its price could be. Unharnessed power of any sort – and especially of this magnitude – he found too frightening to contemplate. Mr. Everett began to withdraw from the world around him.

Everyone thought the cause of his distress was that he simply did not want to move, to leave his land and his yam vines and his cocoa trees. Unlike others, who started out bereaved but changed their minds as the departure approached, getting into the spirit of excitement that prevailed, Mr. Everett became more and more morose. They were a little surprised at his about-face, for he normally took the leading role in everything, a position that everyone acknowledged as his by right, as the only lettered man of his generation. Despite his age, he still had a lot of steam; enough to work in his fields from sunup to sundown, to boss his wife and children around, to have a couple of drinks with the other men, to indulge in chat and rambling arguments with Bailey, his friend and neighbour – and, let it be said, lifelong rival – and still find time to watch all the little girls around as they matured. He was also the first to feel them up when they came to ripeness – another secret, or so he thought. He loved young girls more than anything, believed they were put there to warm his blood. Wasn't there the example of the Old Testament patriarchs, he asked himself.

Mr. Everett was a deacon in the church located on the flat-lands some miles away, having been chosen because of his long and faithful attendance, his reading ability, the clarity of his speaking voice, his mastery of words. The status he derived from it also gave him his greatest protection. If, over the years, any of the girls, down to his own daughters, dared to turn an accusing finger at him, he knew it would be always his word against theirs. He derived a great sense of security from the resonance of his vowels as he read the scriptures, from the straightness of his back as he walked to and from church with the village's largest Bible

– gold edging, the Lord's words in red letters, highly coloured illustrations from the Holy Land, and a Concordance – in his hand and from the way God had blessed him by providing him with healthy children, animals that multiplied and a good sense in business that enabled him to buy up more and more of his neighbours' land as they failed.

He had every reason to feel proud and upright, until the day he was confronted with the possibility that secrets could be exposed and knowledge revealed without one word being uttered. There were new tools in the world that he had never dreamed about or believed possible, a new type of Science greater than the Book of Revelations or even of de Laurence – he had recourse to that occult publishing house from time to time, another of his secrets – and it was this knowledge of a vast, powerful world beyond the mountains, over which he could have no control, that undid him.

3

Everything Mr. Everett did in his life had its shadow side. His church affairs were balanced by his dabbling in sorcery; his respect in the community as the model father masked the despoiler of little girls; the community's honest broker was balanced by a long career of clever cheating, even of Bailey, his credulous lifelong friend who, in Mr. Everett's mind, had now turned into his worst enemy. In a way that even he knew was irrational, he blamed Bailey – the messenger – for the news, for proudly taking him to see, for the first time, the box that proved not to be the beginning of anything but which instead signalled the end of his comfortable existence. So profoundly affected was he by the revelation that he carefully wrote down the date in his big family Bible, as if it signalled a birth or a death: 6th June 1960, which, only on later observation, revealed itself to him as 666, the mark of the Beast. By then it was too late.

The beginning of the end of his reign as king of his little world was in fact many years in the past, right after the end of the Second

World War. First came the rumours. Then came the surveyors,
the white men in their bleached khaki shirts and shorts, wearing
polished boots and pith helmets like all the other bushas before
them, their black assistants wearing soft felt hats, barefooted,
carrying the instruments. Suddenly they were everywhere, tramp-
ing up and down, crawling up the hillsides and fording the rivers.
Testing, they said, to see if the soil had bauxite.

It was a new word that soon became magical. The mountain
people tested it on their tongues, gingerly at first for it was hard
to pronounce, then boldly taking possession of it, absorbing it
into their lives as they and succeeding generations would in time
absorb into their bloodstream its dust and residue, proudly
exhaling it at every opportunity: "Box-hite, box-hite." Over time
the word became talismanic, as simple poor farmers just like
them – though ones who lived in less remote areas than they did
– found their red soil turning to gold. The bauxite companies
bought their land, giving them what seemed large sums of money
so they could move elsewhere, and many of them and their
children were abandoning any pretence at farming to take jobs
with the company.

Though the people of Mr. Everett's district lived too deep in
the bush for any of that fabled wealth to reach them, their heads
were once again filled with events that were mere legends to
them: tales of instant wealth, of men lighting their cigars with
hundred dollar bills, as they had done in the heady days of the
building of the Panama Canal, of the Cuban sugar boom, of the
banana barons.

Then one day, the miracle occurred: representatives of a
bauxite mining company came to buy them out.

Bailey, like everyone else, was bursting with it. "All of us will
be rich," he crowed. "Rich from the bauxite. Look at that Elder
fellow there. Poor as church mouse one day, living in Town and
driving up and down in a car and smoking big fat cigars the next."

The foreigners came in and bought up all the land, all the
farms, all the wilderness, all the ruinate that hadn't been cultivated in generations. Chopping down everything with their big

machines, sending the treasure they extracted from the red
. earth down to the coast by train and from there to Canada and
America, where they turned it into a bright shiny thing they
called aluminium. Bailey loved that word, too, though it took
him – like everyone else – a long time to get his tongue around
it. "Ill-loom, e-loom, aloom-i-nium." Bailey thought it was all
a huge joke and he repeated it every day, laughing and slapping
his thighs. "Imagine, this land bony like mule back, pure hill and
rockstone, and look here, something valuable in it all the time,
eh Dave? Look how long we been sitting on treasure, man, and
we never know!"

Bailey's land and Mr. Everett's had been side by side since their
great-grandfather's time, small plots bought by former slaves.
But while Mr. Bailey's plot had grown by small increments, over
time Mr. Everett's had spread to encompass much of the district.
Mr. Bailey was not envious of his friend, for whom he had the
greatest admiration; he respected Mr. Everett's shrewd dealings
which had enabled him to amass wealth – even the ones at the
expense of others, for Mr. Everett was generous in lending with
interest, and tough with repayments.

If certain families in the district were less than enamoured of
Mr. Everett, they never showed it. Everyone tacitly understood
that such good fortune could only be acquired with the assistance
of higher powers, and nobody was fooled by his churchgoing.
The more charitable – or fearful – attributed these powers to his
superior learning and what came with that. His father was the
only one of his generation who had insisted on sending his son the
five miles to the nearest school, right up to sixth class, and then
paid the teacher for extra lessons. English language and math-
ematics were the teacher's strong subjects, and Mr. Everett came
to excel at both to the exclusion of almost everything else. But
what he had was enough. People always needed him for the
everyday assistance required of someone with book learning: to
read and write their letters, to fill in and sign forms, and other
dealings with the outside world – dealings which also gave him a
great deal of useful information about his compatriots.

The strange thing was that until his introduction to the box, Mr. Everett himself hardly went into the outside world, having little curiosity about it. He left his home only for the most pressing reasons; Bailey or Mrs. Everett handled many of his transactions in the town. Other than everyday purchases, his business hardly involved money. Mr. Everett did not trust banks; he had his own secret hiding places. He loved secrets, and he loved money – or rather, he loved the feeling of power and superiority that his possession of land and cash gave him. Unlike Bailey, he had lofty thoughts; he had no need to go off to the outside world to seek amusement and novelty. Everything he wanted to satisfy him was close to hand, although the requirements of maintaining his various activities – whether rooted in lust or avarice, in the visible or invisible world, in fighting off the forces of envy or conjuring good fortune – left him little time, and demanded his close, unwavering attention. Rising to the challenge of manipulating a web of activities both clandestine and open made Mr. Everett a cautiously happy man – though from his carefully cultivated demeanour of dignified seriousness, even with his family, no one would have known it.

Mr. Everett also loved the secret powers he was able to drawn on, powers to be harnessed and put to work on his own behalf. He had no interest in selling or parading his services, as did those he considered inferior conjurers, obeahmen or herbalists who applied themselves not to the higher Science derived from books but to what he considered old-time superstitious practices brought from Africa by the slaves and handed down unrefined. He had learnt, while still a young man, that while God's blessings, like rain, fell on the just and the unjust equally, there were other forces abroad that could be harnessed by the clever individual for his own gain. Granted, success in this life meant entering into pacts regarding one's disposition in the next – but what did one care when that event was likely to be a long way off? As long as one kept the spirit messengers fed and happy with daily offerings of their favourite food, gifts of rum, tobacco, and the occasional blood sacrifice – marked by the disappearance of one of Mrs.

Everett's white fowls – as long as one carefully read the signs from that other world – the strange behaviour of a lizard, an egg with a double yolk, a green branch suddenly falling – and took the necessary steps to avert disaster, the ultimate payment could be indefinitely postponed.

4

Mr. Everett often thought that even the way he had acquired his knowledge of the other world signified his being chosen.

In his early years of being the good churchgoer, he rejected all those who were whispered to be stealers of souls, traffickers with the devil; he even went so far as to forbid his own wife from securing their services when she, like others in the district, felt the need. He would take down his big Bible and wave it at her, reminding her of the Lord's warnings against fellowship with devils.

But in 1927, his twenty-seventh year, Mr. Everett soon found himself making his own bargains with the Prince of Darkness. The gift of magical arts were provided by a Syrian peddler, Mr. Mahmoud, who every three months or so made the trip up the steep mountain paths, bent almost double with the huge pack on his back filled with goods that everyone looked forward to gazing at and purchasing through his generous extension of credit. It was destiny that on Mr. Mamoud's very first trip, he – worn out perhaps by the unfamiliar climb and a persistent cough – had chosen to collapse on no other doorstep than that of the Everetts'. Forced to stay a while, as Mrs. Everett nursed him back to health, he gave Mr. Everett the opportunity to drink in the words of a man with a superior knowledge of the world, having travelled it widely. Mr. Mahmoud, who disclaimed knowledge of the arts himself, filled his ears with universal tales of power and its possibilities, and arranged to furnish him with all the books and supplies he needed – at a steep price for, as he frequently reminded, they had to be imported and sold clandestinely beyond the eyes of the police.

Strangely enough it was Mr. Mahmoud who, though in a somewhat fragmented way, also supplied Mr. Everett with another, one might say contradictory, source of power. He brought, from time to time, copies of the *Negro World*, Marcus Garvey's newspaper, which he used, like other papers to wrap up his more delicate objects. Mr. Mahmoud got into the habit of handing the crushed-up newspaper pages he no longer needed to Mr. Everett, with some offhand comment about reading about "the scamp" or "the black agitator".

"Read it and be thankful you not where people have to listen to this man and his rantings day and night, Everett," he would say in his mild voice. "A very dangerous man." Mr. Everett never knew for sure if he said it with a smile or smirk on his face, for he found that Mr. Mahmoud embodied in his person such a mass of contradictions, he was impossible to read. He was also never sure whether Mr. Mahmoud sincerely believed he was – as Mr. Mahmoud first said – a man of intelligence and discernment who deserved to be exposed to the greatest knowledge known to mankind, or a credulous fool to whom he could sell some high-priced objects beyond the means of anyone else in the community and books that no one else in the mountains could read.

But Mr. Everett spent little time on such speculation. His brief contact with Mr. Mahmoud was the most important and stimulating event of his life, and he was soon wrapped up in the intricacies of acquiring arcane knowledge that promised enormous rewards. At the same time – from what he could extract of Marcus Garvey's teachings, out of the crushed and torn newspaper pages which he came to read and treasure as much as the expensive books – he was acquiring a knowledge of the historical realities of the world that astonished him. Nothing of the sort had ever been taught in school or at home.

At first, in his excitement, he genuinely tried to share this knowledge with Bailey and other people around. But no one wanted to know about the six million Africans torn from their homes and brought to the New World as slaves, or of the slave past of their forebears, or indeed that it was time for black men to

free themselves from mental slavery. Nobody liked being described as "Negro", "African" or "Black". They saw none of it as
relevant to their lives. Mr. Everett's compatriots sensed the past
only as a dangerous, sleeping forest monster best left undis-
turbed. He himself had been no more knowledgeable or aware of
those matters than they, but now that his eyes were opened, he
felt for them at first a sadness at their inability to comprehend
their own situation, then an anger that hardened into contempt.
If they were content like animals to work from sunup to sundown, to go to the church and sing of being made whiter than
snow in the white man's Heaven, then that would be their
lookout. Mr. Everett intended to take care of himself.

He now saw his growing acquisition of land and power, his
personal aggrandizement, as a kind of reparation due on behalf of
the two centuries of powerless slaves. This belief gave Mr. Everett
liberty to do just as he liked, to use and abuse, to throw off
whatever bonds he chose while tightly binding others, to explore
his own personal freedom to the fullest. Ironically, it was Garvey's
call to the black man to elevate the race by acquiring business
know-how and setting up black-run enterprises that gave Mr.
Everett the justification he needed for his actions.

5

From the time the bauxite company's representatives first came
around, Mr. Everett felt an uneasiness he could not name; and as
it became evident that their mountain community was to be
swallowed up like the others, his anxiety increased. He sensed a
floodgate was being opened to the world that would ultimately
drown him, rob him of his powers. At first he voiced some of his
reservations to his friend, to everyone, but in the face of their
happiness, their desires, he began to say less and less – as if even
he had come to acknowledge the reduction of his hold over them.
And after his dream, the last he was to have, he said nothing on the
subject.

Mr. Bailey was a good interpreter of dreams, and people had got into the habit of coming to him for help. Before the coming of the surveyors, before any disturbance of their bush from the outside, people were dreaming a lot. Not having dreams was regarded as a serious sign of illness or mental disarray, so when people began to wake up with no remnant of a memory of anything that had taken place during sleep, they were taken to Mother Williams, just as if they had a regular illness, and their dreams were conjured out of them with bush baths, whippings, or prayers, as the case dictated. But under normal circumstances, people would come in the cool of the evening, after the day's work was done, to tell Bailey whatever dreams they regarded as exceptional. Such, they knew, were messages from the world of the spirits and meant to be taken seriously.

The last dream Mr. Everett had was so disturbing, so full of ambiguity, that he couldn't wait for evening. He rose at daybreak, drew on his clothes, and before his wife handed him his coffee he dashed over to Bailey's house.

Bailey was just sitting down to his own coffee. His wife poured Mr. Everett a mug too, but it grew cold, so caught up was Mr. Everett in the retelling of his frightful dream.

"I dream," he said, "that I see a lake red like blood and children just dropping out of the sky right into it. Like little angels falling. Mi dear sah, I so frighten I start to cry and I running like a madman to try and drag the children out before they drown. I run and run but is like the more I run, the more the lake getting farther and farther away and more children falling in. I finally reach to the bank side and imagine my surprise, I find many big people already standing there, standing right there and doing nothing, though it look like the lake spreading, getting bigger and bigger but is as if the land shrinking back from the lake as it grow and the people just laughing and shouting every time another child fall in. They laughing at me too for I rushing up shouting: 'Blood! Blood!'

"'A nuh blood, you fool', they telling me. 'Is gold. Won't do a thing to the children.'"

Mr. Everett said he woke up in a sweat, crying; he hadn't seen any of the children come back out of the lake. What really bothered him was the red-like-blood. He knew, as did everyone else, that dreaming of red was a most dangerous thing.

But Bailey laughed and slapped his knees and said, "Why your face long down so? And you have such a good-good dream?"

Mr. Everett was shocked at his friend's response; without waiting to hear more, he put on his cap and stomped out. He never dreamed again – but then everyone had stopped dreaming. No one noticed, not even Bailey, for the entire population now saw a reality awaiting them that they regarded as better than their dreams.

Even though Mr. Everett left in a huff, Bailey continued to laugh. He was sincere when he said he liked the dream, and said as much to Mrs. Everett later that evening by the croton hedge. "Well, it tell me that this bauxite thing coming in now is a good thing for us. Will mean a new life for our children. Is like they get baptise. Born all over again. No more of this hard life, Miss Dell. Concrete house and electric light in our future."

Mrs. Everett said amen to that; like all the women, she couldn't wait to say hello to a life of running water, electricity, comfortable beds, and indoor kitchens with proper stoves.

It was a good thing that Mr. Everett wasn't present because he would have got angry with Bailey and his "foolishness". He could no longer bear to hear Bailey or anybody else talk about the bauxite companies and "progress", couldn't bear to hear of another homestead abandoned by another family. He refused to think of what lay beyond the day when they too would have to say farewell to the land and move.

Everyone said it didn't matter; they could buy more land elsewhere. But why, asked Bailey, would they at their age want land anymore? What he wanted was to buy one of the concrete houses in Town, as all the older folk were doing – and as Mr. Everett ended up doing too. He didn't see the point of anything else.

6

Shortly after Mr. Everett and Mr. Bailey signed the papers for the
land sale, they went to Town together. Bailey insisted they make
a special trip out to where the bauxite works were, so they begged
a lift in a truck there and back just to see.

Mr. Everett was stunned by the sheer immensity of it all,
astonished to see what they were doing to the land. Ripping the
soil up, tearing everything down, leaving nothing but a flattened
red wasteland in their wake. He didn't care what valuable thing
they found in this soil. He didn't understand why they had to do
anything to the land but cultivate it. Why instead of destroying it
they couldn't just assist people to make the soil rich again, make
it fat and flourishing, for nothing was wrong except the soil had
got thin and weak from so many generations of cultivation. If
people carefully nurtured their soil back to health, they could all
live comfortably on the land.

Not even when Bailey took him walking in the new suburbs,
where brand new concrete houses with cars in the carports were
going up every day, was Mr. Everett consoled. "Just look at that,
Davie boy, look at that," Bailey crowed. "That's progress for you.
No more fighting with dirt. Spend yu days with you foot cock up
on your veranda. Spend you afternoon riding around in your
motor car. Ah, Davie mi fren, this is the life."

Mr. Everett didn't say anything. He was furious with Bailey for
dragging him around and showing him all this foolishness, all that
asphalt and concrete and zinc roof seeming ten times hotter than
the farm. What good was it to be a veranda farmer? Was it natural?
"Did God make us to cock up our foot all day?" he demanded of
Bailey. But Bailey only laughed.

After that, Mr. Everett became increasingly short-tempered
with everyone, especially with his own wife and children. He
resented the fact that they couldn't wait to leave behind the walls
made of wattle-and-daub which he whitewashed every year, the
thatch of his roof which sheltered and cooled and protected them.

Except now the thatch was rotting; pieces drifted down all

around them like small, sharp, whirlwinds. It was like that with everyone's house; they were allowing everything to fall apart. The three men who were the best thatchers around had already left for jobs with bauxite companies, and when Mr. Everett asked Bailey to help him repair his roof, Bailey had laughed. "Why bother?" he asked. "When we leaving all this behind?" But Mr. Everett couldn't stop worrying that his walls were crumbling around him. There was no lime to hold them together; no one had time to build lime kilns any more. His wife was neglecting house cleaning, for in her head she had already left. As for the children, they were busy practising Town-speech and manners. There would be nobody left to keep tidy the graves in the little family plots. The graves, like the yam vines, the cocoa trees, the houses, would soon disappear. The bones of their ancestors would be ground up in the red dirt, shipped off to another country to be immortalized in shiny aluminium saucepans and flying aeroplanes.

Could the life force still survive all this, Mr. Everett speculated, after seeing the bauxite works and finally understanding what the end results would be. Would a Canadian housewife one day suddenly find herself unleashing forces beyond her control? Merely by steaming some carrots, heating to boiling point the atom of a human personality embedded in the aluminium born of grave dirt – which in the steam and the heat was so dying to burst its boundaries – would she unleash a force that shattered everything within reach? A force like the invisible ones, familiar to Mr. Everett and everyone else in the district, that from time to time rained down rocks to smash everything within a house, causing the occupants to flee and even abandon their former abode?

Mr. Everett did not care about Canadian housewives and their aluminium pots. What he deeply cared about were the more knowable spirits in the graveyard, some of whom he had occasion to conjure up and consult, and one of whom had become his own personal attendant spirit who guided him in his everyday affairs and protected him from harm.

Trafficking with the spirits, he knew, could only be conducted under cover: away from the light and under the canopy of trees, beneath the screens of yam vines on poles, in the dark and gloomy cocoa walks, or inside the cave in which he hid the implements of his practice, his cash, and his most valuable possessions from prying eyes, and where he conducted his most precious rites. His lustful activities, too, could be exercised away from public viewing, in the bushes or the privacy of his home.

Where would one conceal anything in Town, where everything was illuminated by the full glare of light? Even the houses themselves were boxlike, the white-painted concrete walls reflecting the daylight and electric lights so bright, there was no room for secret fumbling. Their lines were so straight and clean, there was nowhere to stash anything as one could under the thatch roof or in a hollow in the wattle-and-daub. The world to which they were moving, one which harboured no hiding places, was a place of intense danger for one such as he.

7

Mr. Everett had long accepted that one-half of his life must always be lived in the shadow, and that one day the shadow would spread and consume him. It was the price he paid for prosperity. But the revelation of the box in the electrical store – the box that Bailey had said anyone could purchase and enjoy in the privacy of their home, as Bailey himself planned to do – totally confused him. Mr. Everett wondered if that fool Bailey had, even for one minute, considered the implications. He just did not know what to make of it, and his fevered consultations of both de Laurence and the Bible provided him with no knowledge of its provenance. To Mr. Everett, the images inside the box signified only indecent exposure. How did they do it? he wondered. Did they tunnel into people's houses, set up mirrors to reflect their every move? Hide trumpets to broadcast their every word?

Once, he had looked inside the telescope of one of the surveyors' assistants and was shocked at the magic that made everything seem so near. He saw – right in front of his nose – people's underclothes hanging on a line, and had jumped back, startled and shamed at seeing up so close something that should be distanced. Was this box the same kind of thing, a permanent telescope set up to capture one's every move? Could it go backwards and forward in time, reveal past indiscretions? Was it existing only in the now?

Nothing in his life full of secrets prepared him for the idea of such exposure, a light turned on to deeds that were best left hidden, a black box waiting to capture his secret life and retail it. *Everything is for sale now*, Mr. Everett thought bitterly. Paralysed by his own uncertainty, day after day he tried to banish his thoughts, to make his mind a total blank. But then he would glimpse a darkness as deep as the Beast of Revelations, and he believed that if he gazed into that darkness long enough, it might come alive and suck the truth out of him.

The worst was something of which he was hardly aware, so deep was his obsession. His focus on the box was draining him of a sense of obligation to his everyday world, abstracting him from his own reality, making him start to forget the most important thing of all: his daily obligations to other powers.

One morning, Mr. Everett was amazed to wake up and realize that he had neglected to feed his spirits – major and minor – the day before. Although he made sure to make amends, he knew that he had irrevocably set in motion their anger. He had slipped and fallen and needed do something to avert his slide to nothingness – to defer the payment of the final price. But he had already lost control.

Instead of becoming more alert to his responsibilities, more abject in his apologies, and more fulsome in his reparations, Mr. Everett became more neglectful of the spirits that were his lifeline. It was not a conscious neglect so much as a squeezing out of everything sensible from his mind. He felt himself poised at the edge of a dangerous abyss between one world and the next, unsure of what powers he was dealing with, trapped between darkness and disclosure. In his agony he did not bother to call on

the Son of God of the church he still continued to faithfully
support, and to whom he had made many a supplication in the
past; he realized now that this Saviour was probably part of his
present humiliation. Was He not the Prince of Light? He felt
increasingly that the world of disclosure was winning, more and
more worried that his thoughts could be dangerous; if dreams,
which were sent by the spirit world, could simply vanish as theirs
had, where did they go? And if someone had taken their dreaming
away, then waking thoughts too could be stolen, becoming as
dangerous as the spoken.

It came to him then, in a sudden illumination, that it was not
just the land that they had sold. In the papers they had signed, they
pledged their very souls to a power as strong and ultimately as
demanding as the one to which he had long ago pledged his own
soul. In a world where the power to be invoked was not personal
but remote, there could be no control, no appeal; enslavement
was irrevocable. In rushing to bring the black boxes into their
homes, the mountain people were selling themselves back into a
kind of bondage worse, in one way, than that of their ancestors –
for once captured by the box, there would be no hope ever of
emancipation. They would become forever enthralled.

In his last, abiding agony, Mr. Everett felt that if he could
convey this one piece of information to his family, to Bailey, to all
the people getting ready to leave, he could somehow make up for
past misdeeds – in some way redeem himself in this world,
though he knew that his destiny in the next was irrevocable. The
last time he looked into his own eyes in the mirror, the small man
within them had vanished; when next he went to shave he found
to his horror that the mirror gave back no image at all. He ceased
to shave or to do anything considered necessary in this world, for
he knew he was already in transition to the next, where he would
become – as his ancestors had been forced to become in this life
– the slave of another. He felt his body drying and burning from
an inner heat.

He opened his mouth to speak, to tell the living of the dangers
that awaited them, his one great act of generosity and unselfish-

ness that would save them from their doom. He felt a compulsion to tell them everything, reveal his dark and hidden deeds, to convince them of his sincerity and to relieve the great need he felt to confess. He spoke for a very long time, accusing himself of the most vile deeds, even of ones not yet committed. But no one heard. Drained of his will, he had become voiceless. Mr. Everett had entered the box of a permanent darkness with eyes wide open.

THE COUNTRY COUSIN

1

"She can't share our bathroom. She can't," Noelle insisted. "Are you giving her the same towels we use?" She also demanded that Rose shouldn't be allowed to sit at table with them. She was going to be so mortified by her that she wanted no one told she was a relative.

At that stage, Noelle hadn't yet set eyes on Rose.

Noelle at fifteen was all temper. One might have blamed it on her age, were her mother at forty-something not full of temper too. Hot. Hot and saucy. As if the Fennel women had been reared on hot Scotch bonnet peppers, chewed them up raw, though the truth is that only men were allowed to do so. That was a rule that had evolved in the Fennel family, as it had in many others, including that of Mrs. Fennel when she was growing up. Only men ate raw peppers or went bird shooting or walked around the house in their underwear, though Mr. F never once did this because Mrs. F wouldn't have tolerated it, recognizing it as "common". It seemed perfectly natural after her marriage that Mr. Fennel should have on his side plate at dinner one ripe, perfect Scotch bonnet pepper. He would first bring it to his nose as if to test its acrid smell, its temper; he would say "aaah" and look pleased, before cutting it into tiny pieces, carefully disposing of the seeds, then slowly consuming the pepper along with his meal. If he accidentally bit into a seed, his face turned red and his eyes watered – but he also said the "aaah" of contentment many times, something he rarely did otherwise.

The twins would sometimes beg their dad for pepper, and he would carefully put a minuscule bit on each plate. They would mix it up with their food and say "aaah" even when the pepper made them want to cry out and their eyes water, but they never did as they knew men had to learn to eat hot peppers. The girls were annoyed; their father had time and again refused the same request from them; they were older than the boys by many years, and yet from when the boys were quite little, he had had no hesitation in feeding them hot peppers.

"Quite right," said Mrs. F of her husband's actions when the girls appealed to her. "Makes the blood hot." She smirked, as if she knew something more about eating peppers, as if it was some part of that mysterious man-woman thing the girls hadn't yet come to figure out. Granted, Angela the cook always put a whole country pepper in the soup or the stew, but she plucked it out before it burst, as all sensible cooks did.

"Flavour, not heat," Mrs. F loved to explain to anyone who asked, though only foreigners did. That was fine with Mrs. F, for she loved to explain things to foreigners. One of the reasons – perhaps the only reason – she liked going to her Book Club – she hated reading – was that it was full of foreigners, many of whom were attached to embassies. She was frequently asked to their little do's, and she and her husband to some of their big parties celebrating this Day or that Day – something that gave her one up on those poor souls who never got invited to Foreign Missions, as Mrs. F loved to call them.

Though she found the Book Club a terrifying ordeal, she never missed a meeting for she hated to appear uncultured – not just to foreigners but to the refined local women, such as her mother-in-law, who were the backbone of the group. Her mother-in-law had invited her to join the group shortly after she had started speaking to her, and Mrs. F couldn't help feeling, even now, so many years later, that it was not a test, as she had first thought, but a special form of torture the elder Mrs. Fennel had devised. So she was at her Book Club the Thursday evening – having been the presenter for the occasion, she had selected Jane

Austen's *Pride and Prejudice* – when the shocking event occurred at her house.

Over dinner, the girls actually witnessed their father pause in cutting up his Scotch bonnet and, turning to their cousin Rose, newly arrived from the country, say, "For you, Rose?" indicating the pepper.

"Yes, thank you," she said, extending her side plate, on which Mr. F put fully half of the pepper.

When he saw how Rose "demolished" the hot pepper (Noelle's word to her mother later) he called out to Angela in the kitchen to bring another, and he shared that with Rose, too.

Noelle was so shocked that she stopped eating and glared at her father and Rose. When that attracted no attention, she slammed her knife and fork on her plate, splashing gravy, and – giving a strangled little cry, as if she were choking – ran from the room. Had her mother been there, she would have screamed for her to come back, and Noelle would have come back eventually, flinging herself into the chair and putting her elbows on the table to brace her head, letting her long hair fall into the plate. Her mother would have screamed at her and she would have screamed back until Mrs. F would wrap the whole thing up with one terrible threat, which everyone knew would never be carried out, but which was a kind of signature to sign off before they got too tired and ruined their complexions. Tonight, Mr. Fennel merely raised his eyebrows once very slightly and carried on with his meal.

Noelle's younger sister, Simone, was of two minds. She wanted to follow Noelle – she imitated everything she did – but she realized that she had let too much time pass before reacting, so she continued to sit at the table looking down the corridor to see if Noelle was coming back. Her concentration was divided because she was also watching Rose closely to see if after consuming all that pepper she would turn red, choke, and die. Simone knew that would please Noelle no end, but now that Rose was actually here, in the house with them, Simone was no longer sure of her own feelings towards the creature who, before her arrival and behind her back throughout the time she would be with them, was referred to derogatively as "the country cousin". Simone so far had found nothing to dislike about Rose, and now she couldn't help admiring Rose calmly consuming the Scotch bonnet with her meal, doing it slowly and neatly as she did everything else.

Of course the twin boys Jon and Wickie – short for Jonathan and Wickham – had fallen in love with Rose from the moment she arrived and smiled at them. Her actions now merely confirmed what they had already begun to think after a week in her presence: Rose was a heroine worthy of their admiration. Between them they were writing and drawing a tale of a damsel in distress; the name of the brave and battered heroine was Rose, a girl who could take care of herself, beating off demons, hanging on a cliffside by her fingernails, until the hero arrived in a helicopter to rescue her. That would not be for some time yet; they kept arguing whether it should be one hero or two. In one of their earlier books, Rose might have been The White Rose, sister to Guinevere, languishing at home with her long hair hanging out of her castle window while The Gentil Knights went abroad and did battle on her behalf. But King Arthur and his Court had been replaced by Xena, Warrior Princess of television. They knew girls no longer sat at home waiting, but could wander and do brave deeds themselves, almost as good as boys. Soon, they had already decided, they would begin pestering their father for a video camera.

But all this is irrelevant to the fact that when Mrs. F came home with the usual splitting headache, doubled from the Book Club effort and the presence of her mother-in-law, she called Rose into the girls' room – which was where the hot news had been imparted – and forbade her to eat hot peppers. Not as long as she was under her roof, Mrs. F said. That kind of behaviour might be perfectly acceptable where she came from, for standards were understandably lax. But here, in this house, the home of respectable people, ladies did not eat hot peppers.

Mrs. F didn't actually express it in such elegant terms; she reserved such language only for her husband, for her equals, and her betters, as it required much effort, concentration, and a calm demeanour on her part. For Rose, as for the maids, gardeners, and other inferiors, as well as for her children at the very cusp of their annoying her, she reverted – in private, unless she was so upset she couldn't help herself – to the vernacular. So what Rose actually heard was: "Listen nuh, Missis, nuh badda bring yu bad manners here ya; ooman doan heat 'ot peppa, unless dem is gargan; rememba dat; we will hexhercise proper manners hin dis place."

Rose did not look the slightest bit surprised or angry. She lowered her eyes and said "sorry" and looked up and smiled, in a gentle and disarming way. She responded that way to every one of Mrs. F's strictures – and in that first week, there were many. Mrs. F did not know what to do with someone who did not fight back; the only thing she felt confident about in life was winning such battles. Rose made her feel as frustrated as her husband did.

2

That night, Mrs. F sat in her soft silk nightgown, putting moisturising cream on her face. Braiding her hair for the night, she fantasized of tender attention from a dashing, affectionate man; someone – she thought too often for comfort – like Dear Freddie.

Fred Delgado was Mr. Fennel's first cousin and his dearest friend, though at thirty-eight, he was a year or two younger. They often played bridge and sailed together on weekends. Fred naturally had been godfather to Noelle and then to the boys, and was such a favourite with the whole family that even the adults in jest sometimes referred to him as "Uncle Freddie". Freddie was a big booming man compared to Mr. Fennel, who took after his mother's side of the family, which was slim and refined in bone structure and features. Freddie wasn't conventionally handsome. His features were coarse and his gut was developing into a slight paunch disguised by fine tailoring, but his untidy head of black curls, his hearty laughter and bubbling personality were seductive. Freddie was a bachelor – everyone having forgotten one brief and disastrous marriage to an American girl while he was at college there – and the most desirable one around since he was also rich, an only child who inherited a fortune from his lawyer father and was expecting to inherit another from his mother, the heiress of a brewery. Freddie was the brewmaster, a job about which Mrs. F hadn't a clue, but which seemed to her suitably masculine and sudsy, whereas her husband inhabited the drier atmosphere of legal chambers.

Freddie travelled a great deal in his job and frequently entertained visiting Germans and Danes and other exotic Europeans in the beer business, events to which the Fennels were invited. He lived alone and loved to entertain in a very splendid house full of paintings and objets d'art, many acquired on his travels. Despite his business travel, once a year he also took a holiday that would become the talk of friends and family to some exotic place that nobody else they knew had ever seen, like Crete or Indonesia or Tibet. Only after Freddie had gone to such places would Mrs. F hear of other people suddenly going to and talking about them.

"*Fred* Delgado?" Mrs. F would say if anyone mentioned his name in her presence, frowning as if the cat had dragged in something unpleasant; then, after a long meaningful pause, "Oh! You mean *Freddie!*" Thus she would establish their close relationship, while forcing a suitable distance from the speaker. "My *dear*," she would say, "my husband's *cousin* – and *best friend* – godfather to *all* our children, dear Uncle Freddie!" How she loved to talk of *Dear Freddie*, as if she derived exotic sustenance, something bubbly and life-giving, just from his presence on earth.

One of Mrs. F's complaints about her husband was that he didn't know how to enjoy life, though she hadn't discovered this weakness until many years after they were married. Her husband didn't change much, being shy, reserved, soft-spoken, the complete contrast to Freddie who – to Mr. F's eternal regret – was responsible for the only extraordinary thing Roger Quincy Fennel had ever done in his life.

At the age of twenty-one, one Sunday at the beach, Mr. F had gone up to this unknown girl – on a dare from Freddie, for she was by far the sexiest looking creature there, they both agreed – and stammered out some words to her, trying not to gaze at her bosom but trapped nevertheless for he was rather shorter than she.

To this day, Mr. Fennel hasn't the faintest idea what he said; and in the long run it didn't matter, for the woman who would become Mrs. Fennel, waiting for just such an occasion, had opened her mouth and swallowed him whole. That was Freddie's own vulgar explanation of what had happened to his cousin, for it was as if Roger Fennel, in that one careless moment of gazing, had become so mesmerized that he lost all willpower.

He had gazed, she had grazed, Freddie always said; like everyone else, he was appalled at the match. But once Mr. Fennel had made his bed, so to speak, Freddie loyally stood by him as their family and friends fell away. He was pleasant to Mr. F's chosen mate, never dreaming that on that day at the beach, he – being the better known of the two men – had in fact been the target. Had Freddie known, he would have laughed his head off. His contact with one rapacious woman, he always said, had inoculated him against any other. Never would he get caught again.

"Just wait till the right woman comes along," was Roger's tedious response to all Freddie's expositions about avoiding womanly snares.

"Yeah. Right," laughed Freddie, as if that was the end of the matter, though sometimes he could be more loquacious on the subject. Why, just a month or so earlier, in the middle of one of those companionable silences into which he and Roger regularly fell, he suddenly announced: "Not that there is anything wrong with women, mark you, it's just that most of them are so goddamned insecure they end up tearing everything to bits. They've just got to know all the answers and be in control all the time. Being with an insecure woman is like being trapped in a car heading straight for a crash."

Freddie stopped and flushed then, as if his companion could read his mind, for he had momentarily forgotten who it was that was sitting beside him on the stool at the Yacht Club bar. Freddie had actually been speaking of a woman in his own life, one that he regarded as a near miss, and was going to discuss the topic in more detail, when he realized how well his description fit another person close to home. But Roger Fennel had merely said, after taking a sip of his drink, "You're so right," not looking at Freddie, gazing out to sea.

Freddie truly admired his cousin, had done so since they were children; and to that youthful hero worship he had added an admiration of what he considered Roger Fennel's stoic nature. Roger never discussed his wife, never gave indication to her or to anyone of how she might have irritated. Granted that during their youthful all-night sessions in the premarital phase of Roger's courtship, the subject was very much discussed, and Freddie blushed even now when he thought of all the things he had said then to discourage the marriage. But he had stood beside Roger at the altar after all his arguments had failed, and thereafter had assumed his place as a friend of the family.

After a long pause, Roger Fennel now said, "So what is your ideal, then? Has it changed?"

"No, all that has changed is that now I know I'll never find it." Freddie laughed. "A woman who knows who she is, so she doesn't have to tear apart other people to find out."

Now it was Roger's turn to laugh.

Freddie was the magnet of desire for a whole host of women, and he enjoyed whatever opportunities presented. There were always rumours of who had gone along on some of the trips. But, said Freddie, time and time again, never would he be dangling any ring and he made that clear to everyone.

3

At the end of the year, each member of the Book Club had to contribute to the list of books to be discussed the following year. As the time neared, Mrs. F panicked. Her own reading was limited to romances sold in the drugstore, published by Mills and Boon or Harlequin; she knew these would not do. They were far too thin in comparison to those the other women suggested, which were huge tomes between hard covers – chosen for the sole purpose of giving her a headache, Mrs. F was convinced. She couldn't curl up in bed with them; these books demanded she sit up and pay attention. And strain her wrist. But she learned early that she didn't have to struggle through these books; the other women actually read them and loved to show off and talk; all she had to do was open her eyes wide in astonishment from time to time or nod in agreement, turning pages here and there, if a speaker happened to catch her eye. Once a year, however, she did have to speak about the book she had chosen. Freddie always rescued her from the pit of humiliation and despair, suggesting not only the book but often writing something about it for her to memorize.

Mrs. F thought her husband was downright useless when it came to such matters. Instead of helping her as he ought to, his only response each year was to say, "But Rowena, why are you torturing yourself? Why do you insist on belonging to a book club when you have no interest in books?" It was the closest he came to verbalizing a criticism of her, yet it cut to the marrow every time.

"You don't care, do you?" she would hiss fiercely. He blinked as if to clear his eyes, to see her more clearly. Though he had grown accustomed to her shouting at everyone else, he was always surprised when she turned her fierceness on him.

"Of course I care, my dear," he would say mildly. "For your sake I care. I can't bear to see you suffer over anything."

That was the wrong thing to say, for Mrs. F refused to admit that something as lifeless as a book and a bunch of tame women could make her suffer.

"Suffer?" she screamed. "Suffer! *This* make me suffer? Roger Quincy Fennel, you haven't a clue what suffering is." And with that tantalizing remark, and what she conceived as her most deadly look, a full cut-eye, she would swish out, leaving Mr. Fennel to return happily to the peace and quiet of the book he always had his head buried in – Mrs. F's very words which she always said with bitterness, as if the tome was a tomb.

Freddie's quandary in choosing a book was how to strike that delicate balance between something with substance and something Mrs. F could master. But this year, when the question arose, he was over at their house. Noelle was sitting at the dining table, reading the set text for her examination. His eye alighted on it. Jane Austen's *Emma*. Aha! *"Pride and Prejudice!"* Freddie promptly said, raising his hand to make the pronouncement, grinning widely for he considered the title apropos.

As the time drew near for Mrs. F's presentation, Freddie did her an even bigger favour: he presented her with a video of the film, which would save her from the torture of reading. No wonder she considered Dear Freddie the most wonderful person in the world.

4

Perhaps if their mother hadn't gone into such graphic descriptions of poor people and poverty – something Noelle and Simone knew nothing about, but which Mrs. F mistakenly thought would give them a better appreciation of their own fortunate circumstances – they wouldn't have developed such an attitude to "poor Rose." But there it was.

Even before she came, it boiled down to the question of where Rose would sleep. Mrs. F proposed putting a cot in the girls' room, for even with their mess it was large and spacious. It was only temporary, she pleaded.

"I'm not going to share a room with her, I'm not," Noelle had shouted at once. "Heaven knows what we'll get. Head lice and eczema and TB. All poor people have TB."

"TB died off long ago," her mother said in a mild voice, for she was awed by Noelle's knowledge and pronunciation and vocabulary.

"No, it's back," Noelle said. "I read it somewhere." She probably had too, for outside of her school books, Noelle's reading was mainly about disasters, medical or otherwise.

Mrs. F could hold her own with everyone else, but she was putty in the hands of her daughters, who she considered to be so superior to her: in thinness, in colouring, in looks, in brains, in being born into a nice, comfortable home with kind, loving parents. Breeding will out, she often said to herself in admiration of their fine bones, admitting with no hesitation that it was largely due to Mr. F, who was the one who came from the fine family. It was a thought that consoled her when she considered, as she sometimes did, Mr. F's failings. Perhaps it was her obsession with bone structure, teeth, speech, jewellery, crystal, and fine china that made Mrs. F contemptuous about the things that were not fine, most particularly the life that she had escaped from.

She could and did describe poverty so graphically because it was what she herself had known as a child. But she would never have told that to anyone. It was as if, in meeting Mr. F, she had arrived in the world fully blown, in the bikini she wore on the beach where they met and which gave Mr. F a first sight of her extraordinary assets, though it took him long enough to figure that out. She came with no past, except one respectable great-aunt, whom she introduced as her only family, hinting sadly at early orphanhood and vague third cousins in the country.

In thinking of her past, she truly remembered nothing of joy or happiness, generosity or kindness. She remembered hand-me-down clothes and sleeping four to a bed; the stink of urine, leaky rooms, bed bugs, hunger, violent confrontations, dirt, noise, ugliness. She remembered having to toil from sunup to sundown, looking after her younger brothers and sisters while her mother went out to labour at washing other peoples' clothes. Once there had been a father, but he had gone away and never returned, having found an American woman there to marry, they were told by one of his mates. This was the first she knew that her parents were not married.

She cultivated hatred of her mother, her father, the house, her siblings, the life she was born into. As soon as her younger sister was old enough to look after the others, she begged her great-aunt, a maiden schoolteacher in the city, to rescue her. Aunt Vera did, providing her with a home, schooling of sorts, and a model of Victorian manners which was to serve her in good stead.

Yet despite her escape and her lucky marriage – beyond her wildest dreams, beyond genteel but shabby Aunt Vera whom she jettisoned because she knew too much – any thought of the world she had escaped made her anxious. She was given to fainting spells, mouth blisters, sharp and inconvenient headaches, palpitations, neuralgia, high blood pressure, problems with what she called her "plumbing" – though never all at the same time, and from which she was able to recover, depending on what alternative the world offered. She would sometimes scream from her darkened bedroom at the children or the maid, holding both hands to her temples as if to hold some kind of knowledge in: "You *don't* know, you just don't *know.*" She would then pull herself together, telling herself she had to soldier on, dragging herself from bed and getting dressed, if her children were to grow up relieved of the anxieties that weighed so heavily on her.

She had tried so hard to shield them from all the dark shadows that haunted her – like poor relatives suddenly appearing. She couldn't understand why Noelle was becoming such an anxious child, sending that anxiety out in waves that caught Simone in their undertow.

So here was Noelle, screwing up her face while she carried on about Rose. "Why can't she stay in the guest room?" she demanded.

"What! Where would I put my guests?" asked Mrs. F, who never had any, having no family or friends she cared to invite. Her husband's visiting family and friends chose to stay with his relatives.

"The sewing room, then," Noelle pressed on.

"That is the only room in the house I can call my own," said her mother. "Where would you all be if I didn't have my sewing machine?"

Noelle could say nothing to that. They all wore ready-made clothes. The only sewing Mrs. F sometimes did was for herself; she would copy, in the finest and most expensive fabrics, the complex patterns from *Vogue*.

"Why don't you put her in the maid's room with Angela? There's an extra bed."

"Noelle! She might be needy, but she is my own flesh and blood, no matter how distant." Mrs. F had created a greater distance from her niece, her sister's child. "What would people think of me treating my poor third cousin like a maid?"

"The boys' room, then," said Noelle.

"Oh come now, Rose is twenty years old. We can't put her to sleep with the boys."

"Why not, isn't she coming to look after them?"

"Of course not. Where did you get such an idea?" Mrs. F said this indignantly – and guiltily – for that was exactly what she had in mind, though she was not aware that she had ever said it aloud.

Rose was supposed to stay with them for a year while she did a secretarial course. Her mother had swallowed her pride and written to beg, though Mrs. F had let her know, from earlier requests, her disinclination to help – to be, as she herself had put it, "a milk cow". And though Mrs. F's first angry reaction was a firm "No", the request had coincided with the boys' outgrowing their nursemaid. When they came home from school in the afternoon, they couldn't be left alone, but they needed more than a maid or gardener as their companion. They needed supervision and assistance with their homework, someone responsible to stay in the house while Mrs. F went about her business – the girls, of course, having business of their own. The letter requesting help for little Rose was like an answered prayer, though Mrs. F took her time to reply.

"Distant… relatives… country. Poor things. Need help badly," she vaguely told her husband, waving the letter. "Can we see it in our hearts?"

"Of course," he said, as she had fully expected him to say.

5

The twins were eight, five years younger than Simone. Born after a disastrous series of miscarriages, they were evidence of Mrs. F's persistent quest for the eldest grandson and heir of the entire Fennel family. She had already finessed her sisters-in-law by producing the first grandchild, Noelle. Noelle was her Christmas treat, her saviour, her little opener of doors; no one in her husband's family had spoken to her until the birth of Noelle. Having a second girl was a disappointment, but with the arrival of not one but two boys, Mrs. F knew she had clinched it. She could cease childbearing, could even deny Mr. F if she chose, but she didn't, not often, for when all was said and done, Mr. F had stood by her. No question of that. The least she could do. Such moments made her feel big-hearted, generous, giving.

Mrs. F had mentally put down the difficult births of her daughters and the subsequent miscarriages to the strain on her system when she was young and had to carry huge pans of water on her head and so many younger siblings on her back – the source, perhaps, of some of her cries of "You just don't know." In a vague way, she resented her four children for all they had put her through, as if it was they who had insisted on being born, and she envied Rose's mother who had had seven children, one after another, just popping them out – or so Mrs. F, who was not present for any of the births, always imagined.

She pictured her sister as the earthy farm girl, strong, healthy, burnished by the sun, as in the ending of a romantic black and white movie from the forties. Sometimes she voiced these fantasies. "Oh, my country relatives," she would say in a voice implying lovely villas on vast estates. "Life is so simple for them. They don't know, they just don't know. The worries we poor ones in the city have! Traffic! Noise! Facety higglers! Domestics unwilling to live in!" She only said things like this to foreigners.

Compared to how she visualized her sister now – and how she herself had actually been: strong, bronze, statuesque – she saw Mrs. Roger Q Fennel as pale and delicate. She had willed herself to be so once she caught the merest hint, the shadow of the ring closing around her finger. Only her mouth remained to tell the world – from time to time, when she lost control of it – that she was, beneath it all, a gorgon. What she warned Rose ladies should never be.

6

Rose had a gentle and pleasant round face; she was a natural confidante, including to perfect strangers. From childhood she seemed so perfectly centred that she inspired trust in adults. Perhaps her sturdiness helped. Unlike her parents, who were bony and angular, she was tall, big-boned, and well-fleshed as an Edwardian beauty. Rose was sweet despite herself, meaning she didn't set out to be anything and wasn't even aware of the impression she made. It was as if, at her birth, some fairy godmother had come along and granted her the gift to be kind and unselfish. Her sweet nature would open doors, which is why she bore an expression of mild surprise at her good fortune. Such was Rose's aura that people meeting her hardly bothered themselves with the question of whether she was bright or talented, though she happened to be both. It also made people want to help: the teachers who gave her extra lessons for free, the dressmaker who ran her up a dress when she saw her on the road half-naked, the Chinese grocer who always gave her extras and a smile. She never learned self-indulgence, for while still a baby herself she was put in charge of an increasing number of younger siblings.

7

Mrs. F saw none of that when she went to collect Rose at the bus terminus. She drove herself, telling not even her own husband the day of the girl's arrival. She knew he would have insisted on driving her, risking life and worse in that dangerous part of town where the country buses came in. Mrs. F went alone because she wanted no one she knew to see a relative of hers, no matter how far removed, actually alighting from a country bus. She also took the precaution, in case the child turned out to be so awful in looks, speech, manners or, God forbid, all of them, that she would be forced to put her right back on the returning bus. She had come equipped with cash, along with a story of grave domestic crises and a full house in such an awful eventuality.

When she laid eyes on Rose, she felt an intense relief. She wouldn't have to hide her from everyone until she could make her presentable, though her ghastly plastic belt and the red rubber band pulling her hair tightly back from her face would have to go. She was pleased that Rose was well enough turned out and wouldn't embarrass her; she had a pleasant face, a fine complexion, good teeth and limbs, and no immediately visible faults. She was also definitely not fine-boned, which gratified Mrs. F no end. She in fact considered Rose fat and therefore unappealing. While Rose had height, which was one good thing, on the test of thinness, her figure came nowhere close to the girls in Vogue who provided Mrs. F with her yardstick. That rid Mrs. F of one further nagging anxiety. Twenty-year-old girls could be a problem with men.

Rose was unaware that she had passed so many early critical tests on the drive through the city. She was subjected to Mrs. Fennel's first lessons about life: the necessity of secrecy. Nothing was to be said of her family, her past life, her relationship to Mrs. F or anything else. "You might as well call me Mrs. F, everybody does." For Her Own Good.

"Ah, you don't know, child. You just don't know," Mrs. F wound up her homily, beating on the steering wheel for emphasis. "If you give them the slightest little thing, they'll stab you in the back. Trample on your reputation. Beat you into the ground. Turn around and throw everything in your face." Mrs. F punctuated her speech with dangerous manoeuvres in traffic, as if the other drivers were the ones she was talking about, and with exquisite timing suddenly swung right across the street into her driveway. It almost pitched Rose through the windscreen at an oblique angle, giving her no time to ask, "Who?"

8

After much less than half a year with the Fennels, Rose could have answered her own question. She found herself pitched out of the house by Mrs. F, her bag and belongings following, till every single individual item of clothing, or whatever else she possessed was scattered across the paved forecourt of the Fennel's neo-Georgian home. Rose tried vainly to hide her embarrassment as she ran, grabbing items as they fell, not yet sure whether she was more humiliated by the poverty of the items so cruelly displayed or the scantiness of the whole.

Mrs. F saw to it that Rose left with no more than what she had brought. She plucked from Rose's suitcase those items which she herself had given, flinging them in another direction entirely. She never expected to retrieve them, for they hadn't the slightest interest to her, but they helped to underscore her contempt for both Rose and the twice-used possessions.

It was a Saturday afternoon. The audience consisted of the entire Fennel family as well as their maid, Angela. The neighbours possibly heard, but were unable to penetrate the lush Fennel acreage to see. As soon as the altercation moved outside the house, Angela stood off to the side, arms folded across her chest. As it progressed, she boldly stepped forward to help Rose – ignoring Mrs. F's screams for her to go and mind her own business or she'd be fired. The twins held onto each other screaming wildly, "Rose! Mummy!" Noelle yelled and egged on her mother. Simone stood just outside the door, wringing her hands and feeling her stomach contract, unsure which side to be on. Mr. Fennel tried to hold on to his wife to slow her down, an impossibility as she was striding about and waving her arms when she was not throwing things. He said, ineffectually, "Ro, Rowena, please stop. Rose has already said she knows nothing about this. Do not do something you will regret for the rest of your life."

He did not know Mrs. Roger Q Fennel as well as he thought, for regret was not in her vocabulary. In a sense, it was Mrs. F's greatest moment, and nothing would stop her until the last atom of Rose's presence was erased from her house. When she was finished with Rose and her possessions, Mrs. F made sure to wipe her feet on the doormat with exaggerated gestures before gathering up her children as best she could. She managed to enfold only the girls; the twins wriggled out of her arms and laid face-down on the ground, kicking and sobbing. Ignoring them, she swept up what she could of her family into the house, and – barely missing Mr. Fennel as he marched in behind her – slammed the heavy front door.

9

And what had the fair Rose done to deserve such a violent send-off? Had she bared her thorns, turned into a briar, a wild rose, a wolf in sheep's clothing, an ingrate? Or was it the obvious? The middle-aged husband in the same house as the nubile cousin, walking around half dressed, accidentally bumping into him at the bathroom door, waiting to seduce him?

It was Noelle and not Mrs. F who had conjured up such a scenario. She had continued to be dead set against Rose after she came, and over the long run was partly responsible for stoking her mother's fiery personality to the boiling point. It was Noelle who, when her mother had refused to listen to whatever complaint she was making against Rose – for Mrs. F was finding Rose useful – it was Noelle who had fired the parting shot: "Well, you just better watch out. You can't even see what is going on right under your nose."

Mrs. F asked mildly, "What are you talking about?"

"Have you any idea what goes on every morning when they're locked up in that car together?"

Mr. Fennel dropped Rose off at her secretarial school on the way to his office, while Mrs. F drove her children to their schools.

Mrs. F's heart skipped a beat for a moment, and then she recognized what Noelle was doing. Mrs. F herself was not unaware of the potential of the situation – she was too wise a bird for that, she would have said. But she had already studied the two people in question and she concluded there was nothing to be concerned about. Two dead sticks can't spark a fire. So she told Noelle.

"I know men," Mrs. F declaimed, settling down to give Noelle one of her little talks on the subject.

Noelle rolled her eyes, but hung around to listen, having learnt that other interesting information might fall out from such lectures, which were far more informative than her mother intended.

"Men don't go and buy milk if they have a cow. You know what I mean?"

Noelle rolled her eyes again to show her disgust, but nevertheless liked the gross animal imagery, for one of the things she hated about her mother and her cousin was that both were so well endowed in the milk-giving department. She herself took consolation from the models in the fashion magazines her mother kept thrusting at her, but was aware that all the grown women around her, including the ones considered sexy, were considerably better endowed.

"You don't have to worry," her mother concluded, "Your father is the refined type. What would he find attractive in a fat little country girl?"

Noelle did not bother to contradict her mother, not even about her cousin being "fat" or "little", because it would have meant admitting that she had admired or even noticed Rose. Far from men finding Rose unattractive, she couldn't help notice that it was quite the reverse. Her mother, Noelle thought, was stupid. Hadn't she noticed how Uncle Freddie followed Rose with his eyes? Even the twins – usually blind to all but each other and their stupid games – were besotted. And their father was ever so polite and considerate to Rose, which in Noelle's estimation was a bad sign. Indeed, it was this aspect of Rose's presence – her ability to elicit such attention from others without even lifting a finger – that had so infuriated her.

Before Rose came, Noelle had been prepared to ignore her, or treat her with disdain; she had expected an inferior creature in every way, one over whom she could have some control, no matter the age difference. Noelle had learnt from her reading that country people were known to be backward, a condition brought on by debilitating afflictions such as hookworm and malnutrition.

But the Rose who came into their home was not at all the person she had expected. This Rose looked and acted as if she was perfect. And it was as if she had got everyone to believe so, too, especially Grandma. Indeed, it was Grandma's attentions to Rose that motivated Noelle into pushing Mrs. F over the edge.

10

While Mrs. F detested and feared her mother-in-law, she was nevertheless the model for everything domestic Mrs. F did. Old Mrs. Fennel seemed to achieve effortlessly that ease and elegance of manner that Mrs. F envied; she embodied a way of life Mrs. F had always wanted to assume. Over the years, Mrs. F had unconsciously emulated her style in home decoration, china, silver, floral decorations, meals served on grand occasions, jewellery, Christmas gifts, and conversational topics – though of course she had to do everything better and, as the envious said, went right on over the top. Be that as it may, the one area in which Mrs. F had never been able to copy her mother-in-law, her area of defeat, a whole continent in fact, was in capturing an old family retainer.

Mrs. F always pronounced the term with reverence, her voice hushed, her articulation perfect, for Old Mrs. Fennel had not one but several faithful servants, men and women who had been working with her from the time her son was a boy, and who would remain until she or they died. This meant that unfortunately Mrs. F would not be able to inherit them – unlike the family home and everything in it, she hoped – to pass down to her own children, which, in an ideal world, was the way things should have worked. But in the matter of family retainers, Mrs. F sadly realized, she would have to find and cultivate her own.

After every visit to Mrs. Fennel's house – such visits every Sunday had become obligatory since the birth of the children – Mrs. F returned to her own house with both a headache and the fantasy which lifted her out of it: herself surrounded in old age by servants who had been with her forever. Loyal, attentive, and true, cooking and serving perfect meals, dusting without breaking fragile and precious heirlooms, trusted with jewellery carelessly lying about, with the silver, and the most fragile china.

In all her married life, Mrs. F had failed to pin down, much less preserve, such a creature. For some reason, none of the domestics she hired wanted to stay. She blamed it on "the age we live in" which produced girls who were lazy and facety and prone to theft and pregnancy, and young men who were equally lazy and interested in impregnating girls and smoking ganja down by the back fence.

From time to time, Mr. Fennel, worn out by domestic turmoil, would take the initiative and produce someone, usually brought from the country by one of his mother's old retainers. Such a person was Angela, the present incumbent who had been with them for almost two years. Angela would have left after her first week had Mr. Fennel not taken her aside and made her an offer she could not refuse: he would pay for her son's education as long as she stayed with them. Angela swallowed her pride and tongue and stayed, but as she was to tell Rose time and again, she found it "a hard row to hoe."

Mrs. F did not consider Angela ideal for the role. She was too uppity, too quick of temper, and entirely too ambitious, with a son at the best boys' high school, the one Mr. Fennel had attended. Mrs. F hadn't a clue how she managed it on her wages – though she might well be a thief, as Mrs. F fully expected to find one day. The unwelcome fact regarding Angela's son made Mrs. F determined – against her husband's wishes – to send her own sons to expensive and exclusive Canadian private schools which were becoming fashionable alternatives with people in their set.

Up to the time she received her sister's letter, Mrs. F had so inoculated herself against relatives that she had never thought of a country cousin filling the role. But as soon as the possibility of Rose arriving presented itself, she saw it all: the poor but decent cousin who would become the long-serving, faithful house-keeper, renouncing a house and children of her own for the privilege of maintaining the Fennels.

11

Rose ended up sleeping in the sewing room, on a couch Mrs. F had cleared. It was layered with dust, for Angela had been forbidden entry on the suspicion that she would not be able to resist helping herself to Mrs. F's finery.

To Rose, none of that mattered. Having a room to herself was heaven enough. It was an inspired move on Mrs. F's part, because Rose's eyes were immediately caught by the beautiful fabrics, ribbons, threads, laces, spangles that crowded the room. She smiled and said "Oh," and brought her hands together, like a little child, and opened her eyes wide, taking it all in.

"Do you sew, Rose?" asked Mrs. F, watching her closely.

"Yes," said Rose, not knowing sewing involved more than the handwork she had been taught in primary school – good enough for the mending she was often called upon to do – or operating her mother's ancient straight-stitch treadle machine to create the most basic garments.

"Aha," said Mrs. F, clapping her hands. "We'll have some great times sewing together."

It wasn't long before Rose learnt that in such circumstances, Mrs. F's "we" meant "you". She had no time to find her bearings before finding herself engaged in hard labour. Her daily routine became more demanding than her duties at home; there, at least, many of the tasks she did had been left entirely up to her, providing her with some sort of satisfaction. Here, Mrs. F supervised her every move and was often highly displeased with the result – especially with Rose's sewing. Mrs. F was an impatient teacher, so impatient in fact that after a short while she banned Rose from touching anything in the room. Rose was not to look or to breathe on any of her garments-in-progress, for she had, Mrs. F informed her, the clumsiest pair of hands she had ever seen. That did not stop Mrs. F from assigning Rose to assist Angela with house cleaning, ironing, cooking, setting and clearing the table or washing up. Nor did it prevent her from fulfilling the other list of duties: ensuring the boys were fed, dressed, and ready for school in the mornings, and supervising them after school.

Rose did everything she was asked without a murmur, without once losing her gentle speech or smile, but a small vertical crease developed between her eyes. For with all the duties, she was finding it hard to keep up with the very thing she had come to the city to undertake: her secretarial studies. She could hardly find time to do the exercises assigned each day, struggling with them after the others had gone to bed and her own domestic chores were completed, often falling asleep over her instruction book. She was hungry most of the time as well. The only decent meal she had was at dinner, and she never dared ask for more than what Mrs. F served her, for the one time she had done so in response to Mr. Fennel's invitation to second helpings, she had sensed Mrs. F's disapproval. Mrs. F herself ate like a bird and Noelle and Simone only pecked at cooked meals, though like the boys they filled themselves up on snacks and sweets the minute they came home from school. The message Mrs. F seemed to exude and embody in her person was that males could eat as heartily as they liked, but women had to be careful what they ingested.

Although Mrs. F had promised her sister, Rose's mother, that she would take care of all her niece's needs, she didn't think of giving money to Rose. A few days after starting her lessons, Rose was to find herself without lunch money or bus fare and was forced to walk several miles home each day, literally falling through the door and straight into the arms of two little boys waiting to be entertained. It was Angela who noticed her limping home one day and got the story out of her. She promptly phoned Mr. Fennel at work and told him.

The next morning, when Mr. Fennel stopped the car to let Rose out, he awkwardly held out a wad of bills without looking at her.

"Here, Rose," he said.

Rose's eyes opened wide, but she knew better than to take money from men. She looked at Mr. Fennel with horror.

"No, no. Take it," he said, thrusting it at her with some desperation, reading the expression on her face, but even more aware that he wasn't properly parked and was blocking traffic. "Mrs. Fennel forgot to give it to you," he said. "It's for bus fare and lunch."

When still she hesitated, he said, turning fully to look into her eyes: "Rose, as long as you're in my house, I want to feel I can treat you like one of my own daughters. I don't want ever to think of you having to walk home or going without lunch. I want to think you can trust me, and always tell me what you need." And then, still disconcerted by her stare, he added, "My wife, Mrs. Fennel, she means well. But sometimes she... forgets." He hesitated. Rose still said nothing. He began to feel undone by her innocent stare.

Rose, embarrassed at his knowledge of her intimate affairs, looked into his eyes and saw that they were identical to the eyes of her favourite uncle, Noel, who had died the year before. Thus reassured, she took the money. Thereafter Mr. F gave her money once a week, large sums in Rose's eyes; she carefully took out what she needed and sent the rest to her mother. Neither she nor Mr. Fennel discussed the matter; they travelled each morning in a companionable silence.

From time to time, Mrs. F absent-mindedly gave her small sums, but since Rose never asked and seemed to be getting along quite well, it never occurred to her that Rose needed anything. She gave her unwanted clothes from her own wardrobe and approved of how presentable she looked wearing them. Still, she didn't want Rose to look too good.

"No, no, no!" she cried out the first time Rose appeared with her hair let out. She couldn't believe how stunning it made her look. "You look so much better with your hair pulled back from your face, dear Rose. Trust me. You should always wear it like that." She made it sound so much like an order that Rose wore her hair pulled back in a ponytail. The one thing Rose did admire about her aunt was her glamorous way of dressing.

The ponytail made things easier; she had little time to spend on herself, and sharing a bathroom with the girls made it almost impossible for her to worry about make-up or hair styles. Noelle made it as difficult as possible for her to gain access to the bathroom or to spend any time in it. Although the girls left the bathroom in such a mess and a great part of Rose's time was spent cleaning it before and after use, Noelle never ceased to complain to her mother about having to share with Rose, and about things she manufactured.

12

Things might have continued that way indefinitely – Rose was determined to finish her course, no matter what, knowing how much getting a decent job would mean to her family. And it might have worked out the way it was planned, if Old Mrs. Fennel hadn't taken such a shine to her. That – as Mrs. F would have said, had she been asked to identify the kernel of the matter – was what brought the wolf to the door, the straw that broke the camel's back.

Mrs. F didn't consider taking Rose to Old Mrs. Fennel for Sunday lunch, though her husband had asked about it from the start. "Oh little Rose has too much to do," Mrs. F had said airily. Sunday was the only time Rose had to herself, though it wasn't true, as Mrs. F implied, that Rose herself had taken that decision not to join them for lunch. It was Mrs. F who had decided, arbitrarily, that

Rose wasn't ready for exposure to society. Only a few days after her arrival, Dear Freddie had dropped by and been persuaded to stay for dinner. It was the first time he saw Rose, and what a fiasco that was. There was Dear Freddie, being his suave, sophisticated self, trying to make Rose feel at ease. And there was the silly girl, totally failing to respond to any of his conversational sallies, blushing and looking foolish and countrified, not even meeting his eyes when he gazed at her across the table, as he did quite frequently throughout the meal, as if willing her to respond. Freddie, being a tease, had come back quite a few times thereafter and made a point of trying to get a response from Rose, but she continued to keep her head down, raise her eyes, and smile shyly. Mrs. F couldn't stand women who said nothing. Socially, she felt she had to fill every minute of space with something witty and amusing.

Rose's lack of witty repartee had become embarrassing to the point that Mrs. F began to show some petulance in the matter, saying sharply, "My dear Rose, can't you answer when a person is speaking to you?"

But the person in question – Dear Freddie – had been too embarrassed and had looked at Mrs. F with an appeal in his eyes for her to say nothing more, that he understood, warming Mrs. F's heart with his kind and considerate nature. Shortly thereafter he had taken his leave, pleading another appointment, and smiling at Rose to let her know he held nothing against her.

Mrs. F had derived satisfaction from those experiences; while she wanted Rose to fit in and not embarrass her, she certainly did not want her to fit in too well.

Imagine her horror when, as soon as they arrived at Mrs. Fennel's that Sunday, that fearsome lady – after, in Mrs. F's estimation, a perfunctory greeting to her son and his wife and children – had looked around and asked, "And where is the charming Rose?"

"Charming Rose!" What a shock! Who could have told her that? Mrs. F thought wildly, for she herself had said nothing about Rose to her mother-in-law other than a vague, "Poor girl from the country... give her an education."

Mrs. F glared at her husband, who must have been the culprit. There could be no one else. But he showed not the slightest sign of guilt, helping his mother back into her chair.

13

Old Mrs. Fennel took to Rose. Everybody could see that from the minute Rose walked in the door. "My dear, let me look at you," she said, holding her at arm's length. Mrs. F knew instantly what Mrs. Fennel was trying to do. Trying to embarrass her and her daughters, to reduce them to nothing, to treat them like dirt. This time, she decided, she would have none of it. Mrs. Fennel had ruled her life enough. No country cousin was going to spoil things. Not that Mrs. F could see what her mother-in-law saw in Rose. The stupid girl did nothing but nod and smile at everything, barely opening her mouth when people talked to her. But Mrs. Fennel treated her like an honoured guest, on the first visit taking her and showing her around the house and gardens. "What a sweet nature Rose has," she said, in front of the girl. Mrs. F gritted her teeth.

After their first meeting, Mrs. Fennel invited Rose to come over on Saturdays. It became a regular thing; Rose even sleeping over until Sunday. Of course, the clever old witch did not invite Rose herself; it was Mrs. F that she called. "My dear Rowena," she purred in her husky voice. "Can you spare dear Rose? She's so marvellous with my hair." Or, "I do need some company to go shopping." What was dear Rowena to say but "Yes." She didn't own Rose. Rose, as she told her mother-in-law with a laugh each time, was a free agent. "Rose," she'd call out, "Mrs. Fennel would like you to come and spend the day, dear."

"Oh, but I have to…" Rose would start to say, having come running.

"Oh, no, my dear, don't worry about that," she would say, loudly enough for Mrs. Fennel to hear over the phone. "Of course you can go. You are a dear sweet girl to offer, but I won't

have you spending so much time in the house. You must get out
and enjoy yourself."

Rose got into the routine of spending time with Mrs. Fennel.
Many Saturdays a car would pick Rose up and drop her off
afterwards, or Rose would stay the night and return home with
the family after Sunday lunch. Mrs. Fennel sometimes called
for Rose during the week, taking her to concerts and art shows
and God knows what else, for Mrs. F could get only the most
meagre information out of Rose when she returned home.
Rose, Mrs. Fennel kept saying, was just what she needed, such
a delightful companion. Since when did Mother Fennel need
anyone? And what kind of companionship could Rose provide?
In the early days of her marriage, Mrs. F would have given
anything to be her mother-in-law's companion, but she had
shown not the slightest inclination for her company. Noelle and
Simone, when they were little, spent time with their grandmother, but as they grew older they developed other interests.
Only natural, Mrs. F thought, as a good mother who understood child development should. But Mrs. F now thought with
resentment that their grandmother had made no real effort to
ask them to come again.

Mrs. Fennel gave Rose gifts too: scarves, costume jewellery,
and little lacquer boxes which Rose put away as carefully as the
greatest treasures. Mrs. F saw them as she checked through
Rose's belongings from time to time, and was alarmed by the
development – just as she was by finding several thick, heavy
books in Rose's room – but she was reassured that the gifts were
trifles compared to those given to her children.

She didn't become alarmed until one Sunday, when she heard
Mrs. Fennel planning a trip to Europe. Mrs. Fennel declared she
hadn't gone in a long time because, since her husband died, she
hated to travel alone. She was thinking that when Rose finished
her course, she would make a good travelling companion.

Mrs. F could not have been more mortified than if Mother
Fennel had thrown hot pepper in her face. Not that she herself
would want to travel with her, but she had never asked. Rose, to

Europe! Where Mrs. F had never been. Mrs. F wanted to choke. She knew what the plot was now. Her mother-in-law wanted to capture Rose entirely for herself, the selfish old goat, as if she didn't already have all the family retainers she needed. "Rose is mine, mine," Mrs. F wanted to shout, though good manners prevailed, as they usually did in the presence of Mrs. Fennel. But the suppression of her natural impulses so enervated her that it brought on one of her medical crises and Mr. F was forced to take her home before lunch was over and leave her in her darkened bedroom to recover.

This time, Mrs. F remained so upset that she was forced to pour out her heart to Dear Freddie. Her husband was of no use when it came to the matter of his mother. Dear Freddie, whom she had summoned to come for a drink before dinner on an evening when she knew her husband would be delayed, sat in the gazebo with her and sipped his drink as she poured out her feelings about Mrs. Fennel, Rose, and the plot against her household. Freddie wasn't given to saying much in such circumstances, he was too much of a gentleman to comment on a matter that, after all, affected his family too, but he murmured soothingly. Mrs. F understood his reticence and knew he understood, for more than once he had driven Rose home from Mrs. Fennel's – Mrs. F had seen from her bedroom window his car drive up into the courtyard and turn around and drive off the minute Rose alighted. No lingering! At first she was shocked to see them together; then she was disappointed that he couldn't stay; then she understood his desire to be rid as quickly as possible of the country cousin's boring company that, she later learnt, Mother Fennel had foisted on him because she had sent her own driver on some errand and wasn't above calling on Freddie.

Tonight, with Freddie her own captive, Mrs. F – after passing some remarks herself about Rose's inadequacies – told Freddie, as a delicious joke, what Noelle had said about romance developing between Rose and Mr. F. Freddie looked startled, but laughed heartily, especially when Mrs. F said, "My dear Freddie, you know your cousin so well. How finicky he is. How refined his tastes! Paintings! Orchids! Books! Can you just see him taking up with a little country girl?"

Freddie almost choked on his drink. Unfortunately he couldn't stay for dinner. "Business visitors, you know." But as usual he had so enjoyed his little tête-à-tête with dear Rowena. Her view on life was "so original. Would not have missed it for the world."

14

Despite her annoyance, it had never occurred to Mrs. F to get rid of the problem by sending Rose home; Rose was still useful in her household. It was left to clever Noelle and her doomsday perspective to give Mrs. F cause for alarm. Noelle began to bring and read to her magazine clippings of foolish old people leaving their fortunes to cats, dogs, religious institutions, and perfect strangers. Sometimes they married their caregivers, often a fraction of their age, and died the moment they had altered their wills. Mrs. F, considering the implications, felt like swooning. Though Noelle offered no comment, the message was clear. Besotted old people did foolish things with strangers, leaving their own blood relatives in the poorhouse.

Noelle had been well schooled by her mother; Mrs. F had drummed into her brain the fact that their father, as the eldest child and only son, was Mrs. Fennel's main heir, Mr. Fennel senior having left his fortune to her for her lifetime. So there was much to be passed down to the grandchildren. Grandchildren who were especially nice to Grandma. Mrs. F was pleased that her daughter had in fact taken in that one important lesson and was so greatly concerned with family matters.

Had she been able to read Noelle's mind, Mrs. F would have discovered how wrong she was. The whole notion of a fortune was, to Noelle at her age, a mythical abstraction. What really drove Mrs. F's eldest child was simple jealousy of Rose, who had come to represent those parts of herself that were so far missing and that she most desired. Everything might have turned out differently if she had started on another footing, had not developed such a hostile attitude, but the stance she had assumed from the start made it impossible. She had boxed herself into a corner of hostility and loathing, and all she could do was envy the relationships her own sister and brothers had developed towards Rose – her father, her grandmother. Rose had become so much the centre of Noelle's passion that she had no option now but to continue the momentum, to go forward, to push Rose entirely out of the door and back to where she had come from. Only then would she find some relief.

For Noelle, what Rose really demonstrated was how little she could trust the opinions and judgments of her own mother: on the matter of country cousins, Mrs. F had been wrong.

15

Saturday afternoon, matters came to a head in the Fennel household. Mrs. F was already on the boil, just waiting for Rose to come home, for the previous week Rose made the fatal mistake of returning home wearing a little ruby ring that she recognized instantly as belonging to Mrs. Fennel – one of numerous rings she possessed, and of the least value perhaps, but the fact that her mother-in-law had given something valuable to Rose disturbed Mrs. F in a way nothing else had. She did not comment when she saw Rose wearing the ring, but she couldn't take her eyes off it; she had stewed all week since her discovery. What next would Mrs. Fennel give to Rose? The old woman was going mad, crazy, she thought; if one didn't watch her, she would part with all the fine jewellery and everything else that, in Mrs. F's mind at least, belonged to her two eldest granddaughters.

Noelle noticed the ring, too.

"Mom. She's stolen Grandma's ring," she hissed the minute Rose left to clear the table.

"Shh," Mrs. F said, indicating their father. Mrs. F knew that Rose had stolen nothing for she had, in her subtle way, managed to bring up to her mother-in-law the question of the gifts to Rose, and Mrs. Fennel had brushed them off as "trifles". Mrs. F knew in her heart that the ring, too, was a gift, but she didn't bother to disabuse Noelle of the accusation. An idea began to form in Mrs. F's mind. What the gift of the ring finally told her was that Rose, no matter how useful, would have to be sent away, and in such a manner that she would be disgraced in the eyes of the entire Fennel household so that no one, not even Mrs. Fennel, would show the slightest sympathy. Rose would have to be shown up as a traitor to the family, an abuser of kindness, a thief.

Mrs. F got the idea of planting one or two pieces of her own jewellery, a piece of silk, and a few other small items that could be carefully hidden among Rose's belongings when she was out. She planned the resulting exposé for a Saturday afternoon when Mr. Fennel was home, as she wanted him to witness at first hand Rose's treachery.

When the twins came home from school that week with head lice and Noelle found out about it, she started screaming hysterically at her mother. "It's Rose! You see what I mean? Why did you have to bring her into our house? You see what you get for that?"

Mrs. F said nothing; she saw it only as additional fuel to be added to the fire. Mrs. F didn't bother to tell Noelle that the school principal had sent a letter to parents – excessively apologetic, for it was the most exclusive prep school in the country – to say there had been an unfortunate outbreak at the school but they had traced it to its source and taken the appropriate steps to prevent a recurrence. Mrs. F had already screamed in person and down the phone to the principal, assistant principal, school nurse, chairman of the school board and sundry board members – of whom her husband was one – as well as to a number of increasingly higher officials at the Ministry of Education who refused to allow her to speak to the Minister. By the time Noelle heard about the problem, by way of the twins screaming from Mrs. F's rough treatment of their scalps, Mrs. F already had the matter well under control. But now it suited her purpose to allow Noelle's hysteria to flower fully.

16

What more is there to be said? Picture the scene yourself. The driver drops Rose off and she enters the house without noticing the ominous silence, an air of expectancy. Picture the father, left out of the scene so far, happy in the backyard, tending to his orchids, never suspecting what drama is about to occur. The heroic role he will ineffectually play.

It begins with Mrs. F's discovery of the loss of two rings and a string of pearls from her jewellery box. There is noise and confusion; the house is turned upside down, putting Angela in a huff. She is the first one to be asked if she has seen the jewellery, and so she feels accused. But Angela stands her ground in a belligerent pose, her hands folded over her ample belly. She asks: "Is what I would want with your things, Mrs. F?" Indeed, she does not look like someone wishing to drape herself in diamonds and pearls. Mrs. F, thinking of the son in the expensive school, almost begins to believe she has really lost her jewellery and it is Angela who has taken it. But Mrs. F quickly pulls herself away from the fantasy of firing Angela.

"Come," she says, sweeping all four children out of the bedroom and down the corridor to Rose's room. She needs witnesses. "There is just one place left to look. You come too, Angela," she says.

"I want witnesses," Mrs. F declares, pausing dramatically, hand to her heart. "I never want a single soul to say I lying."

Triumphant, Mrs. F clutches the purloined items in her right hand as some world-class actress playing Medea might have clutched a dagger. There is a pregnant silence. The twins are too stunned to say a word.

"Jesu, lover of my soul," Angela moans under her breath.

17

And so Rose is driven from the Fennel household, in a much noisier atmosphere than the one that greeted her. She and Angela have stuffed her things into the suitcase and Angela is trying in vain to get the old lock to hold. The sight of that broken lock seems to be the breaking point for Rose; she starts to cry, stumbling over to a rock that is part of the landscaping on the edge of the forecourt. Rose makes no attempt to wipe her tears away, she sits up straight with both arms at her side stiffly holding on to the rock as if she needs to balance herself.

"Don't cry mi darling," Angela says. Having given up on the suitcase, she turns her attention to pressing Rose's face against her body and holding her.

Rose just sits there, every now and then saying in a wondering kind of voice, "I never took anything. How Mrs. F could say I take her things?"

"But don't me know that?" Angela asks indignantly. "Everybody know. Rose, don't bother yourself, ya. You better off going home to your mother. That woman is poison."

"But now she's going to tell everybody I'm a thief. And I never steal a thing from I born."

This realization brings a fresh round of weeping, which is interrupted by the surprise appearance of Mr. Fennel, jangling his car keys. "Come Rose," he says, bending down to lift up her suitcase with both hands and putting it in the car. He turns to help Rose.

They hadn't noticed the twins, who watched the scene, and who now rush to Rose, clinging to her, sobbing and calling out her name. Rose bends down to give them one last hug and Angela has to pull them away from the car and keep hold of them, one on each side of her, as Mr. Fennel drives Rose away.

18

When Mrs. F heard the car start up, she looked out her bedroom window and saw, with consternation, her husband driving off with Rose. That was not in her script. She had wanted to see Rose stumble down the road with her suitcase, humiliated, finding her own way to the bus station and home.

Mr. F's behaviour was unexpected. Mrs. F was upset. Instead of being disgusted with Rose's behaviour, he had disapproved of his wife's. As soon as he had entered the house he had given her such a tongue-lashing! It was the first time her husband had openly showed disapproval of her, and in front of the children, closing his argument in Rose's favour by saying he could not and did not believe she had stolen anything. Furthermore, even if she had, he found Mrs. F's treatment of Rose to be unforgivable. She'd been embarrassed and humiliated, and so was he. At that, Mrs. F had rushed upstairs to her bedroom and slammed the door. Then she had prepared herself for a negotiated reconciliation.

It was to be the longest evening in her married years, for Mr. F did not return. Many hours were to pass. The hours exposed her to her darkest fears. What if what Noelle had hinted at was true and Mr. F had now run off with Rose? That it was she, Mrs. F, who had driven him into the little schemer's arms? It was unthinkable.

Yet there was his strange behaviour toward her, his wife. Wasn't that evidence enough? He had clearly expressed a preference for Rose over her, hadn't he refused to believe her version of events? Hadn't he driven off with Rose? Hours and hours ago. Frantic, Mrs. F got on the phone, to call his mother, sisters, Freddie, his office, clubs, all his friends, whoever she could think. The answer was always the same. No one had seen Mr. Fennel.

Much later that night, when her nerves were at breaking point, Mrs. F saw her husband drive in. She hurriedly got into bed and pretended to be in a deep sleep. She did not have courage to ask him where he had been all that time. The fact that he had returned was all the reassurance she needed.

19

All of these events tested Mrs. F severely. But the event that was to change her life forever, the worst piece of treachery she was to experience – so she told herself – was the fleeting half-smile she caught on her husband's face. Not the day she had driven Rose from her house – that day she would always look back on as a day of triumph.

For a while after Rose left, she was able to bask in the satisfaction of knowing that Mother Fennel had not once asked about Rose, and Mrs. F herself would not dignify the subject by bringing it up. It was enough that Rose had sunk back into dirt and squalor and oblivion. Mrs. F had learnt her lesson, which was one she knew her own daughters had also fully imbibed: never have dealings with country cousins.

It was the thought of Rose's eclipse from Old Mrs. Fennel's consciousness that kept Mrs. F going, for she now had to fill spaces left in her household. Angela had summarily departed, thanking Mr. Fennel for all his help, but not even her son's future could keep her tied to such a post. Mrs. F was kept busy hiring, firing, hiring, firing, and scrapping much of her own activities, for now she had to spend time at home with her sons every afternoon. She was so busy that she hardly had time to notice Freddie hadn't been in touch.

"Travelling," was Mr. F's laconic response to her question. She fleetingly thought that her husband seemed more silent and withdrawn than usual, but she attributed it to his fortieth year fast approaching. She was well aware of what *Vogue* had to say on the subject of men and their midlife crises, the subject having been exhaustively discussed at the hairdresser.

With a start she realized that it was time for Dear Freddie's annual holiday trip. He could not have gone already – every year without fail he had come around with the brochures and maps to share with them the chosen "exotic locale" in Mrs. F's words. The event was followed by a flurry of postcards. It was Mrs. F who encouraged Freddie to share his trip with them, for she took the opportunity each time to try and interest Mr. F in travel.

"Bali," Mrs. F would breathe, eyeing in full colour brochures beaches very like the ones of her island home. "What wouldn't I give to go there! Roger, look at this."

But all she ever got out of Mr. F after he had muttered "Ba-lee" under his breath was: "You all can go if you want. You know how I hate to travel."

Mrs. F would look at Freddie then, wishing him to open his mouth and say he would take her, but of course he never did. And since there was no point in travelling without a husband, Mrs. F's travels were limited to shopping trips to Miami with other women, something she regarded as social defeat on a massive scale. Every year when Freddie brought the brochures she would hope, and then when that hope was dashed, all she had left was a fantasy of herself looking pale and thin and elegant, playing the leading role in the pictures she had just looked at, her head resting against someone who could not be clearly identified but whose hair was dark and curly.

So imagine then Mrs. F's feelings when, some five or six weeks after the contretemps with Rose, a huge, thick, square envelope arrived addressed to *The Fennel Family*, in Dear Freddie's own handwriting. Mrs. F's heart palpitated before she noticed the stamps from foreign parts. Freddie, she thought sadly. Gone on his trip without a word. Mrs. F ripped open the envelope to find a photograph and a thick square card. One look at the photograph and she could have fainted dead away. She was fortunately not overcome, with nobody around to help her. She managed to totter over to the settee, lying across it for a long time with one arm flung over her eyes to shut out the light. Her first thought was she had suffered critical eye failure. When the darkness cleared, she picked up the photograph again and held it up close to her nose, still believing her eyes were playing tricks.

It was *her*, with her head so close to Freddie's it seemed their hair was intertwined, for hers was no longer pulled back in a ponytail but stylishly fluffed up and loose.

Mrs. F found it too much; she fell back on the settee and closed her eyes for a considerable time, moaning loudly, "Lord. Oh, Lord," wishing she had someone to fetch the smelling salts.

When next she sat up to take in another element in the picture – for only in this piecemeal manner could she absorb the totality of the information it contained – she noticed first the blueness of the skies, the white houses on the hill in the background. They were sitting at a table outdoors in an exotic locale. She was wearing a low-cut dress of what seemed to Mrs. F's discerning eye to be of the finest silk. Around her neck, bronze against the white silk, was a large and perfect string of pearls. It caused Mrs. F, without thinking, to grab and rip from her own neck the pearls her husband had bought her just the Christmas before. These now seemed the puny offspring of dieting oysters.

Mrs. F let out a wounded cry from deep inside her belly when she recovered herself sufficiently to look at the picture a third time and notice that she and Freddie actually had matching grins. Why hadn't she noticed that before? It would have given her a sign! She would have known immediately which way the wind was blowing and nipped it in the bud. Mrs. F groaned when next she caught sight of the size of the glittering ring on a bronze finger. She fell back on the settee.

It was much later that she remembered another stiff piece of paper had fallen out of the envelope. She bent to retrieve it – a mistake perhaps given her delicate state of health, for this was to complete the devastation to her structure from which she never fully recovered.

It was a marriage announcement: *Miss Rose Geraldine Purcell. Mr. Frederick Royston Quincy Delgado. In London, England.*

Despite herself, Mrs. F was forced to make a rapid calculation of the date and discovered it was a mere three weeks after Rose had left her care and protection. Now the questions arose to haunt her, to which she was never to obtain satisfactory answers. Had Rose gone straight to his house? The slut! To live in sin? Did his mother know? Oh, my God, she lived in London, England. Old Mother Fennel? Could she have known what was going on all along? Was it her doing? Why Rose of all people? Is that why Mother Fennel never asked a single question about Rose? Mrs. F couldn't stop the questions spinning round and round. Roger? What role had he played in all this? Where had he taken Rose that night? To Freddie's? To Mother Fennel's? What exactly did he know?

Mrs. F tottered to her bedroom, holding Freddie's missives in her hand as if they dripped poison. She drew the telephone to her and tried to dial her husband's office number but was so distraught that she found she had completely forgotten what it was. She fell on the bed and worked through her anguish by clawing at the pillows till she ripped them apart, coming to her senses long after to find downy feathers covering the bedroom like foam.

Mrs. F always rose to the occasion. By the time her husband came home that evening, she had cleared away every sign of turbulence in her person and her home. As if adversity lent her new energy, she had cleaned the house, cooked, bought new pillows, soaked in a long bubble bath, and put on her sexiest white dress that showed off her efforts at the gym and undimmed natural physical assets, the perfect setting for her heaviest gold chains and earrings. She was made-up and calm, ready to greet Mr. Fennel with the news. She had already decided to say nothing to the children for the time being. Maybe the children need not know, she thought wildly, for never would those two darken her door again. If this was some sort of conspiracy against her by the Fennel family, she would show them. If the Fennel family wanted to ruin the lives of innocent children by their treacherous behaviour, then on their heads it would be. She would endure it with a dignified silence.

Unfortunately, there was a time lag between such resolve and her husband's arrival, and so it was no fault of hers that her earlier thoughts and anxieties came crowding in again to upset her delicate balance. No doubt the others were involved, she assured herself, but not her Roger; Roger would never keep secrets from her, she would bet her life on it. Roger was the only person in the entire human race she could trust. Hadn't he kept his word that he would marry her when she told him she was pregnant, when any other man in his position would have found a way out, for that had been her experience. It wasn't her fault that she had, in fact, made a mistake, but he had never once thrown that in her face. No one could say she hadn't made Roger a good wife. Where would someone like Roger have been without an energetic woman like her to push him? What if he had married one of those puny, pale-faced girls his mother would have chosen for him? What kind of children would they have produced? The thought of her fine, strong, children made Mrs. F feel so mighty at that moment she could have chewed up the entire Fennel family – including Freddie D, whose mother was a Fennel – and spat them out in little pieces. Except for dear Roger.

Mrs. Fennel awaited her husband in the bedroom, not wanting to alarm the children with the news. As soon as he loosened his tie, and before he had time to do anything else, she held out Freddie's missives, glad that she had not followed earlier impulses to rip them to shreds.

"Roger, we have news, my dear," she said gaily.

She deliberately handed him the picture and invitation face down, so he was forced to turn them right side up to see what they were. The picture came out on top. She watched him very closely, as closely as she had ever watched anyone, as he glanced at the photograph before holding it up to the light to look more closely. So she was able to capture on his face that fleeting smile, before he wiped it off – a smile that was to become imprinted on her heart, never to vanish.

He knows, she thought. *He knew all the while.* He instantly recovered himself and expressed due wonder and surprise. But Mrs. F never heard what he said, so deep was the wound of his treachery. It pained her so much, she lost all the control she had so carefully cultivated; what she said or did, she could not remember afterwards. In any event, after that, it didn't matter. Nothing could ever be the same.

FLYING

1

His father had bought him a return ticket, first class at that; but, as the plane banked sharply for its descent, he wondered if airlines reimbursed for the portion unused in case of death. He knew he would never return on that ticket. He was twenty-six years old and he had come back to the island to die. His father didn't know that, although he had recognized he was ill enough to warrant the comfort of first class. He was touched: his father was normally tightfisted. Perhaps he did know. Perhaps everyone knew. Family, friends, strangers on the street. Everybody knew but nobody wanted to know.

After the long flight, it took his remaining strength to walk to his mother's car; he moved so slowly that she had to slow her pace, though she was in high heels and he towered over her by a foot. He was glad to discover she was a woman without curiosity. She didn't comment on his slow movements, his grey pallor, his thinness; she'd been told he'd been seriously ill with pneumonia and complications when he'd called to ask if he could come to stay for a while. She'd said yes without hesitation. But now he thought her very casual in her greeting, considering she hadn't seen him for twenty years. When she first sent him to live with his father in Canada, she had kept in touch with the occasional letters and phone calls, but as he grew older the connection had weakened, both of them seeming to lose interest.

But she had said yes when he'd asked if he could come. To him that was the important thing, though he had no idea what he was coming to. He knew of the material changes in her life, but in his mind he still associated her with the simple mountain home he'd left behind. Now, as he eased himself into her Mercedes Benz and watched her beringed and manicured hands on the leather-covered steering wheel, her beautifully styled hair, and her made-up face, serene and confident, purposefully set straight ahead, he began to understand that in acquiring a whole new life for herself – a well-off husband, three other children – she had no need of him. Perhaps, he thought, she had never needed him; perhaps he had been nothing but an interruption in her life, a slowing down of her upward trajectory, a burden she had shed.

He never knew why she had decided to send him, at the age of six, to live with his father in Canada. Or – his father's version – why she had suddenly consented to let him go, after years of his father's pleading to have him. But even as he assumed a new life with his father and stepmother – for whom he was an only child and on whom, for a while at any rate, they had lavished their affection – he increasingly felt a vital piece of himself had been jettisoned.

2

In his mother's house – an architect-designed bungalow in a smart new suburb – his stepfather and his three half-brothers seemed huge and bursting with energy. The boys, all teenagers, had been told he was ill, and were happy to leave him alone, popping into his room to say "Hi," when their mother reminded them of his presence, just as happily dashing off, bouncing their balls in the corridors, shouting on the telephone to their friends. Their father was pleasant and solicitous, but clearly unsure how to deal with him, the child his wife had had when she was seventeen – long before she had dreamed of moving to the city and becoming his secretary, then his wife.

They took to referring to him as "The Sleeper", jokingly to his face. At first he was startled – it seemed such an accurate description of his life – then realized it had started after his mother told them the story of something that happened when he was a child. They were sitting around the dining table, one of the rare days he felt well enough to join them, and it was his mother who brought up the question of his sleeping so much.

"Don't you remember, Jonathan, the day you fell asleep at guava tree root? In the middle of the day, just like that?" she asked.

Everyone laughed, but nervously, as they did when he was around. He kept his eyes on his plate and said no. "What do you mean?" he asked. "What would I be doing at 'guava tree root'?"

He winced as he heard in his voice imaginary quotation marks around the colloquialism and wondered why he felt such hostility. But greater than his surprise at harbouring such feelings was his surprise at feeling anything at all; worse, at not being able to keep from showing it. More than anything else, he took this to be the true measure of how far his illness was taking him away from what he had construed as his true self: masked, secretive, self-aware.

His mother, whose mind always seemed to be rushing head-long towards another topic before she had finished with the first, didn't appear to notice. Nor did anyone else; it was a household in which nobody seemed to focus much but on their own preoccupations.

His mother surprised him by asking, with a laugh in her voice, "What, don't you remember how you loved guavas?" She turned to the others, looking at each boy's face in turn as if seeking his confirmation of her veracity. "You know the little river below YaYa's house?" she asked them. They all nodded.

"Well, in the old days, when there was plenty rain, the bank was covered with bush and guava trees. Not like now, when it's pure rockstone.

"The joke about Jonathan was that from he was big enough to walk, every day he wanted to go down to the river bank to pick guava. After a while he didn't want anybody to come with him, this is his way of showing us he's a big man, you know, getting up and down that hill by himself." She paused to laugh and threw her head back, showing her beautiful teeth. Then she turned and spoke to him directly.

"I would stand on the hill and watch you, and by now you knew enough to throw away the guavas with worms. That's one thing you were fussy about. You could only eat the perfect guava. I don't know... It wasn't that you were greedy, more like finicky, but you'd search and search, picking and examining every guava till you found it. The one that was good enough for you. You'd stand there and eat it on the spot, turning it from side to side as you bit into it, chewing it slowly. Then, when you were finished, you'd fill your pocket or your cap with guavas and bring them for me and YaYa. You were so serious about the whole thing, I'd laugh myself silly every day watching you as you scrambled back up that hill, trying not to lose the guavas you were carrying."

"Then what happened?" he asked, for it seemed she had suddenly lost interest in the story, turning to offer her youngest a second helping, then shifting her attention to her own plate.

She put down her knife and fork again and smiled, but as if from a distance. "One day, you went looking for guavas as usual. I wasn't at home then – this is after I got the job working with Father Donohue at the rectory so I was away all day. YaYa was minding you. Poor YaYa, you gave her such a fright I don't know how her heart didn't burst! She watched you go down the hill and start looking for guava. YaYa says one minute she is watching you, the next minute a plane is flying right overhead. She lifted up her eyes to look at the plane and by the time she looked down again, you were nowhere to be seen. She called and called: 'Jonathan! Jonathan!' Not a peep and she can't see you anywhere. She almost broke her neck running down that hill. Her one thought was you'd gone into the water. She started looking around. No sign and now she's shouting out for help, till she finally reached to a part of the bush far from where she saw you. She couldn't believe her eyes. There you were in the sunhot, lying on the ground. Dead to the world. At first she thought something had happened to you, that someone had carried you off and hurt you, but there was no sign of that. Up to this day, YaYa will tell you she can't figure out how you could reach so far and drop asleep in that short space of time. Sleeping so soundly she couldn't wake you. She had to carry you up the hill and put you to bed, though it was the middle of the day. Jonathan, you slept for twenty-four hours straight, sleeping the sleep of the dead. You don't remember?"

The fact that he couldn't remember didn't matter to her or to the others; in the minute it took him to marshal his thoughts for a reply, they had lost interest and were chatting of other things.

When he got his mother's attention again, and asked her to tell him if they had learnt anything about what had happened to him that day, she suddenly seemed unwilling to continue. "No, you never remembered a thing, got up the next morning and came to the table and had your tea same as usual. We asked you, but you didn't know what we were talking about. Of course you were only a little boy – though it was right after that that the trouble started." She said the last bit almost to herself.

"What trouble?" he asked, pouncing on the word.

"Oh, nothing," she said, embarrassed about the whole thing. "It had nothing to do with you, just... trouble... in the district."

He would have persisted with his questioning; it was suddenly so important to him he could feel his heart fluttering, but she looked at her watch, said she had to be off, and practically ran from the room.

In a way he didn't mind; her story had left him feeling almost elated. He wanted to sit quietly with it. The story itself seemed trivial; for all the importance she had imbued it with in her telling, he couldn't remember what guavas were. But he held close to himself the image of a child who was so closely watched by two women; a child, he told himself, who must have been loved. He wanted to cherish the story as the first he had heard in which he was the actor, a contour line drawn.

3

The story triggered a memory not of himself, but of a place; brought into focus a picture of a little stream and its green surroundings, a piercingly sweet aroma and something mysterious and strange hovering just on the edge of the picture.

This vision of the cool, lush riverside kept coming back and helped to dilute his first disappointment upon arrival. There were no forest-clad mountains meeting the sea, as he had seen in the pictures of this tourist paradise; no lush rainforests, but a land that was dried to brownness, the hills bare and scarred from bush fires, the city itself covered in an ashy haze, all seeming as stricken as he was. No rain had fallen for over a year and even the lawns of the wealthy were dried dust bowls, the only colour the brilliant scarlet bougainvillea running riot, an affront.

But from the moment his mother told the story, he had glimpsed an opening in the haze, a window into cool rainforests, the smell of damp earth and mossy coverts. He knew the place now: it was his grandmother's home in the country, the place where he was born, and where he spent his childhood before he was sent away. He understood for the first time why he had so wanted to return. It was not to be with his mother, as he had thought; it was simply to get back to his grandmother's place.

4

His mother had promised to take him to see his grandmother, but kept putting it off. Each time he reminded her, she made excuses. Once she said, "YaYa's place won't suit you. You grew up in Canada with modern conveniences, Jonathan. Your grandmother refuse to change her ways. You know how many times we offer to bring her up here to live with us? Or build her a nice house? YaYa refuse to change a single thing in that house. She and all those little old people down there she spend her time with, they're all living backward in time. It wouldn't suit you at all."

He spent hours lying on the bed with his eyes closed, though he wasn't sleeping. Sometimes he didn't have the energy to get out of bed; sometimes he didn't know why he should bother. But after his mother told the story about the guava, he increasingly felt that he needed to harness what energy he possessed – for what, he was not sure. Perhaps one day some grand final effort would be required of him and he needed to be prepared.

Like something in a story, his grandmother suddenly appeared. He saw an old woman walking ramrod stiff up the driveway, a felt hat jammed down on her head, numerous bulging, wayward parcels badly wrapped in brown paper and tied with string dangling from her hands. He knew immediately who she was. He felt his heart stir, urging him to lift off, to fly straight into her arms. But, before he could marshal his wasted body for the move, she had already entered the house through the kitchen door and, dumping her parcels along the way, walked straight into his room.

"Come, I tekking you to my country," was her only greeting, making it sound as if she lived in another country entirely and not in the mountains of the next parish, some thirty miles away. She began to drag his cases from the wardrobe and pack his clothes. This seemed perfectly natural, though he normally wouldn't have stood for anyone touching his things.

As soon as his mother came in, YaYa commanded her to drive them to her home. His mother began to make excuses.

"Awright, we tek bus," YaYa announced, grabbing up one of the bags. "Come, Jonathan."

He was amused to see that his mother was embarrassed by YaYa and her country voice and ways, for her city-lady voice became sharply pronounced.

"What! You'd take Jonathan on that old country bus?"

"Mi spirit just tell me to come for the boy," YaYa said stubbornly.

As if knowing she could not win this fight, his mother heaved a sigh and parcelled them up into her Mercedes. She drove them to YaYa's country and left him there.

5

In his grandmother's small wooden house, lying in the same room he had lived in as a child – and he was pleased to have recognized it as such before she told him – he idly watched a trail of ants crossing the unpainted board wall and wondered what the ants were saying to one another when they met and stopped. As he had this thought, a funny feeling came over him. It was as if the skin of the earth had ruptured while he stood on the edge, and he had almost fallen. But over the last few months, he had learnt that his body was capable of these warning signals of something off-kilter. Soon he felt all right again.

The land here too was parched, the mango tree outside his window miraculously bearing a few straggling leaves. A single bird spent much of its time perched in it. He didn't see any other birds and assumed they had died off or retreated to the high forests, for there were no bird sounds. Coming from a geometri-cally laid out city of high-rises, he was amazed to see how soft the edges were here, how nothing seemed to have been trained or groomed, how no one thing stood out. Everything – from the mountains to the country road and its high banks – wound in and out, twined on or enfolded something else. Even YaYa's little house had long abandoned its vertical lines and settled comfort-ably into the soil, its foundations masked by the roots of pepper-mint and leaf of life, thyme and sinkle bible and croton, which she worked to keep alive.

YaYa's house seemed as tiny as she was. He, who in another life had been so proud of his height, now kept bumping into things and hitting his head on the lintels, feeling as if he had grown too quickly and thoughtlessly and uselessly, like a shoot covered in debris, stretching its pale self to reach the sun. That thought made him aware of the paleness of his thin body. He started to sit out in the sun each day, wearing only his shorts until he turned nutmeg brown like his grandmother. That didn't stop him from feeling as useless as the sun-deprived shoot; the yard was as far as he could walk. He smiled every day he heard the shy little boy next door singing at the top of his voice as he herded his father's cows, over and over like a dirge, as if this was the only fragment of song he knew: "What gaan bad a maaning cyan come good a evening, woi."

6

He was at first embarrassed that he could not help his grand-mother, but she brushed aside his protests. He got the feeling that even if he were fit, she would not have handed over to him anything of her daily routine. Part of that routine was walking a long distance to collect water. He was fascinated to watch how economical she was in using it: a calabash-full served for a bath. But then she was economical about everything. Her hands had never known waste, he thought. How profligate was his life!

It was YaYa's view that the drought was not accidental, but a punishment for the wickedness of mankind. In the old days, she said, people kept the flow of water regulated by making sure that due reverence was always paid to Rivermaid, the guardian of every fountainhead. When angry, Rivermaid withheld her bounty. So in former times of drought, huge processions would make their way upstream to her residence at the source, to offer prayers and sacrifices. YaYa claimed that in the old plantation days, so her Granny had said, the Massa would sometimes allow them to sacrifice a whole ox to Rivermaid, so water would flow to turn the sugar mills again. Her own church members were nowadays the only ones who kept faith with the water spirit. When Brother Jeremiah the Water Shepherd pumped away till the spirit washed over him and flooded the room, Rivermaid triumphantly entered to possess her followers. But Rivermaid had not revealed herself for a long time now, no matter how often the Revivalists travelled in a body to the pool from which the river emerged, to try and contact her. Her displeasure had not lifted despite their offerings: white fowls and rum – all they could afford. Perhaps a greater sacrifice was required.

Jonathan wished he had something to offer his grandmother that would make Rivermaid surrender; he felt guilty that he had come empty-handed and needy. YaYa had taken him on as her burden and he didn't know why; she hardly knew him, but her entire day was spent seeing to his needs. In addition to water, she foraged for the right food, searching for just the right bush to relieve his itch or bathe his aching limbs. She fed him like a child, she bathed him when he was too weak to manage himself, she made it clear she expected nothing of him. He had never imagined or experienced such close attention from another human being. And, just as he began to enjoy for the first time the feeling of trusting someone, of letting go, so he also felt his guilt increase. The guilt he had felt all his life for his inability to commit to unconditional love. He had sleepwalked through school, university, jobs; always without focus, as if he expected to meet his real self along the way. He knew now that everything he had tried was to fill that emptiness: sports, TV, the encyclo-paedia. And other things he decided he didn't want to think of. Part of his life lived in the dark.

Now he was hiding the biggest secret. From his father and stepmother in Canada, from his mother and her husband, from anyone he had ever known; revealing nothing had seemed the only way. He didn't want to die abandoned and alone.

His grandmother was different. It was not just her kindness that moved him; he sensed in her a kind of sorrow, of fulfilment suspended, an absence akin to his. He felt a deep responsibility to her that he had never felt for anyone before. More and more he felt the urge to tell her exactly what was wrong with him; he wanted to speak truth, to utter its name. He wanted to tell her that he was a danger to her, a curse. That what he found unbearable was this love that was breaking out in him.

7

One day when he was too weak to get out of bed and she had brought him soup, he paused with the spoon halfway to his mouth and said, "YaYa, you know what's wrong with me?"

He was shocked when she said calmly, "Yes, mi son."

"What?" He couldn't believe his ears.

"Jonathan, you don't have to tell me nothing. I know."

He didn't know how to respond. He fell silent.

When he finished eating and she was clearing up, she said: "You know why this happen to you?"

He shook his head.

"Is because Father teef yu spirit."

"Father?" He thought she meant his own father. The minute the plane had disgorged him in Toronto, he had forgotten everything of the six years that had gone before.

"Father Donohue. Your great-grandmother Tano give you this gift and is your mother make Father Donohue tek it weh. From that, nothing never go right."

"What do you mean?"

"You nuh remember?"

"YaYa, all I remember is living with you and Mom here. Nothing else."

His grandmother looked thoughtful. "Fancy that," was all she said. She pulled the blanket over him and blew out the lamp. "Rest now."

8

It was a long time before they talked again. He had a bad spell in which he thought he would die, but his grandmother's ministrations pulled him through.

One day he said, "YaYa, you're more than twice my age and I am going to die and leave you when I should be the one taking care of you."

She said calmly, "You might reach there before me, that is all."

Now he had got used to her bush baths, she had taken to wetting his head and body from time to time with a foul smelling substance which she called Spirit Weed. She ignored his protests, saying only, "Is to protect you from evil."

"YaYa, you don't understand," he cried out in anguish one day. "The evil is inside me."

"No," she said. "Anything you have only get inside because something leave you, something they take away. But we can get it back."

"Get what back?"

"Yu rightful spirit."

"How?"

"You don't mind how. Trust them that know."

He wondered who those were. The two old men who were always hanging about, her friends Bro Nebo and Bro Samuel? But even more urgent than that was the question: how could she have known that all his life he had felt a part of himself was missing? He had never discussed it with anyone. And who were "they" who had taken his spirit away?

Sometimes, after listening to her, he felt as if he was rapidly falling backwards into a zone where anything was possible. He wondered if he was hallucinating from his illness or from the stuff his grandmother kept giving him to drink. Whatever it was, it was making him feel better. He was beginning to believe there was something in her bush medicine, in her bush baths and in the bitter tonics she brewed and made him drink several times a day.

She herself would go off into the hills to search for medicine: one day she announced it was time, folded her crocus bag inside her heng-pon-me basket, grabbed her machete and left, returning hours later, the herbs and roots, leaves, berries and bark filling the crocus bag which she carried on her head. He never knew what secret signs told her a particular leaf was ready to be plucked, but precision governed her every action. As he sat on the kitchen stool and watched, she would carefully count out the leaves or berries to be thrown into the pot of boiling water, measure a piece of root against her hand and cut it to the length before pounding it in a mortar. Some items she put in the enamel basin by the window. "That must wait for three day," she would say. Or, mixing several ingredients together she would place them in a dark cupboard. "That take seven day to ripe." By the time she was finished apportioning each day's harvest, all was accounted for, nothing was thrown away.

Everything, she said, all her knowledge, came from High Massa through her grandmother, Tano, who was born with second sight and became a noted Warner Woman, her mouth a megaphone predicting disaster, her urgent dream messages commanding her to wrap her head in fourteen yards of coolie-red with a pencil stuck in the seventh fold, bind a seven-foot long cord around her waist with her scissors looped through to cut away evil, take up her Bible and staff in her hand and walk to warn people within whatever radius she was ordered to go, be it one mile or a hundred. Traversing the countryside, through towns and cities, she would stride at a furious pace, except when commanded by inner voices to herald the whirlwind and spin counterclockwise, waving her Bible and staff and loudly proclaiming disaster and devastation on the populace unless they repented and mended their ways. Her message concluded – and the people appalled by the apparition, for many of her warnings came true – she would return home to assume a normal life at her yard, practising her other gift, that of healing.

YaYa would proudly talk of her grandmother Tano and her gift. Then she would seem to run out of steam and get a sad look in her eyes and fall silent, before abruptly busying herself with some task. But one day, she didn't stop talking until she came to the source of what Jonathan had read as her sorrow.

"When she getting old, Jonathan, she want somebody to carry on the work. She want this gift pass down in the family line, for she herself get it from her mother who get it from her father, and he was a real African who come after he learn all these things over there. In Africa." YaYa said this with such pride it made Jonathan smile.

"Well," she continued, "they waiting for the sign now, but time pass and none of Tano children get choose, so she couldn't pass on the gift. When I come born with the veil they know is I am the one get choose."

For the first time since Jonathan had known her, YaYa, looked discomfited, twisting the hem of her apron between her hands.

"Ai, Jonathan, if only I did know what a precious thing it was," she exclaimed. "But I was a wayward child. Mi parents did hand me over to mi grandmother for training so I live with her and she start learn me, about bush and herb and all the treatment. Same like her, is through dream mi spirit come and tell me what wrong with the patient and what to use for the cure. But see here, is mi waywardness mek me break the chain… dream never come to me again… is only a little about bush I member now… and I never receive the last gift."

"What was that?" he asked.

"Yu wi see," she said. "Maybe it pass down to you, for after me, it was you in the family get choose." He began to ask about this, but she continued, "Then again, maybe the gift was meant to pass away. Maybe the world too change up."

He knew it was no point pressing her, so he asked what she meant by her waywardness.

"It was a hard life," she said. "Nothing but work and studiration. I mean study with Tano for I never get no schooling like the other children. All I learn to do was count and measure. Tano was very strict. And I used to see all the other little children around playing and I envy them so much. For I was really a small child, you see, but I had was to behave as if I was big woman. Everything strict, strict. No joking and laughing. Maybe I did come without conviction for I envy those other children so much, my heart was not really in it and more and more I neglect my duty. When Tano die, the Yard die from neglect, for there was nobody to carry on. I forget everything. I get married, have my daughter. I wanted was to live like other women." She shook her head. "No wonder everything just fall away from me."

"What's 'everything' YaYa?" he asked gently.

"You don't see?" she asked in surprise. "Mi husband. Mi daughter – mi only child. Mi precious grandson."

She said it so passionately that both of them stayed silent for a long while.

"Well, mi daughter, now..." she finally said, musingly. "You see, I make a big mistake with her, big mistake. Though maybe it all work out for the best. For you see her there now in her big house, driving her big car, looking so please with herself, how else that would happen if we never hand her over to the nuns to get education? Mark you, I never did want to take that step. It never seem right for our family. Is her father. Him see what they doing for the young people around, how so many learning to better themself and right away he want that for her."

YaYa paused and stared into the distance, wiping her face with her apron and letting out deep sighs before she continued, "Deep in my heart I didn't feel right about handing her over, but I never go against my husband. And I have to say they did teach her a lot, all the things I never know, so I couldn't give her and they send her off to boarding school and she there getting along good, learning shorthand and typewriting, plenty subject, studying for her exam. We expect the nuns protecting her; how we to know she sneaking out to meet this man? Big man old enough to be her father? Well, at least at the end of the day he do right by you, Jonathan, him own up to him responsibility. She never even know him is married man with wife in Canada till she tell him she making baby."

Jonathan said nothing, drinking it all in.

"That was a disappointment all right, and then mi husband go and die just before you born," YaYa continued. "But you know what?" she said, smiling for the first time, "When you born into mi hands was the happiest day in my life; mi heart just rejoice, for you born with the caul, same as me. When I see that, I feel seh Tano forgive me, she never desert the family after all. Is through you, Jonathan, Tano send back the gift."

The gift! Jonathan lifted his head in anticipation, expecting to hear the mystery revealed. But YaYa simply continued with her story.

"Mark you, for a long time I don't sure. So I watch and pray for guidance. Is only when you four – five, that day after you fall asleep down by the river that I sure. It was right after that you start to prophesy. Just like Tano."

"The day I fell asleep?" He was alarmed at how fast his heart was beating.

"You mean you remember?" His grandmother seemed excited.

"No, Mom told me about it. YaYa, you know what happened to me that day?"

"No, but it was right after that you predict Thomas' death."

One day, said his grandmother, he was standing with her out by the road, talking to a neighbour, when Sawyer and his assistant Thomas came by. They greeted everyone as they passed and the boy suddenly screamed, "No. Thomas don't go!" and rushed after the pair, screaming and bawling and trying to hold on to Thomas. Everyone was surprised at his behaviour for he was normally a quiet, well behaved boy, but he wouldn't stop screaming even when she gave him a few good slaps. Sawyer and Thomas went on their way, shaking their heads.

Later that evening there was a great commotion and they rushed out to see a tremendous crowd of people coming down the road, carrying a makeshift stretcher and the body of Thomas lashed to it.

"What happen?" YaYa asked.

"Thomas get into accident with the saw," they said.

"Him dead?"

"Yes."

YaYa told Jonathan she went inside the house, feeling strangely troubled. By that time he was in bed, fast asleep. She stood looking at him for a long, long time. When his mother came home and YaYa told her what had happened she begged her not to tell anyone.

"It's just coincidence," his mother had said.

"Yes," said YaYa.

In the aftermath of the funeral and mourning, nobody remembered the boy's strange outburst until one morning when, instead of drinking his cocoa, he lifted his head, looked at the wall for a good long time, and then said, "Mrs. Williams dead."

"What you say?" she had asked.

"Mrs. Williams dead."

She had looked at him. She asked him, gently, "Son, how you know Mrs. Williams dead?"

He looked at her without answering.

"You sure?" she asked, and he nodded. Later that day, she heard Mrs. Williams had dropped dead that morning. She told his mother, who again begged her to say nothing.

But the third time the boy predicted a death, there were witnesses and before the corpse was cold, the news had spread. People began to gather in their yard to look at him and discuss the matter. Since she wasn't the one wanting to hide the boy's gift, she chatted freely.

"Well, he is his great-great-grandmother Tano's child."

Jonathan heard how after that his mother came home every day in tears, having to force her way through a crush of people to get into her own house. She cried, for she didn't want a son who had second sight or anything that seemed out of the ordinary. His mother was ashamed when she, YaYa, talked of Tano and such things she knew Father Donohue would have described as the work of the devil. But she couldn't stop the flood of people and the talk, and soon their house became a shrine with folks coming from far and near to see this amazing prodigy. They tried to ask him questions but the little boy only yawned and said nothing. His gift was one of foretelling death – nothing else could be cajoled out of him. The predictions came spontaneously, or so it seemed, usually too late to prevent the fated occurrence.

YaYa was in her element, appointing herself gatekeeper and regulator. She put the boy to sit on a huge cushion in the armchair so that he could be seen. She dressed him in white from head to toe. She made him a turban of silk. She never charged money but she accepted gifts people brought, mostly food until there was so much she gave most of it away to the needy.

This went on for some months. YaYa kept waiting for something else to be revealed, for his gift to be converted into a force for healing, for that was their family calling. She should have expected it, she told Jonathan now, the day his mother came home and would not look her in the face as she told her Father Donohue was coming to take the boy. He was possessed of devils which had to be cast out. He would stay at the rectory till God's work was done. The priest would come for the boy in his car at night so as to avoid the crowd.

"You remember anything, Jonathan?" YaYa asked hopefully. But, like everything else, he had no memory of it. "I never know what that man do to you, the time he have you there," she said, sounding very old. Then, angrily, "I don't care what anybody say, when them send you back, you not the same boy. Is like everything just drain out of you. I will never forgive your mother for letting you go. Never! I forbid her, but she was stronger than me for she threaten to leave and take you. I know they would help her. It was me against them. What I could fight with? When they had you there, they wouldn't let me through the gate when I say I come to bring you soup and clean clothes. I stand there in the road in the broad daylight and bawl the living eye water. You see, it come to me that if I wasn't so wayward and did stay with Tano and learn what I was put in this world to learn, it wouldn't go easy so. For I would have power, you see. But I was frail as a lamb. And I never have a soul to help me. You know the hardest thing? I never know that she would still send you away. Oh I was blind!"

As she talked, Jonathan was overcome by a memory of blackness, of flying black clothes, of language cutting the air like a sword, he felt something escaping from him with a hissing sound, and then a feeling of falling, falling into a tunnel, into a kind of blankness. He must have fainted as he recollected this, because he came to and found himself crying, a deep and desperate sobbing for something lost.

9

Jonathan realized what had happened to him, and he began to
understand his grandmother's insistence that his sickness was
absence, not presence – not something added but the result of
something that had been taken away. She believed that if something had been taken, it could also be replaced, but he was not so
sanguine. None of this knowledge made him feel that his illness
could be cured. Not even the best doctors in the world were
holding out that possibility. She compelled him to retrace his
steps, to fit together the puzzle of his life.

He began to wonder what really had been taken from him by
the exorcising priest, for he did not consider the ability to predict
deaths a particularly valuable gift. There must have been something more, something he had received as a bounty. His grandmother clearly had no knowledge of this, but he felt that the loss
was greater than any of them had imagined.

More and more his mind wandered to that day by the river
when he had fallen asleep, for whatever had happened there was
the key. Whenever he tried to picture the scene, something always
hovered on the edge of his consciousness, just as it had when his
mother had told him the story. "It will come back," voices
seeming to come from the air kept saying. "It will come."

10

Despite its sadness, YaYa's story added to Jonathan's growing
understanding that he was part of something. He was born not
alone, as he had always felt, but had fallen headlong into history.

He began to fade away. One evening YaYa lay on the bed beside
him and cradled his head on her breast as if he were a little child.
He couldn't help himself; he started to cry. She hushed him and
crooned a song, and then she told him a story.

"Now," she said, "I will tell you of the gift. The gift I might
have had if I was not a wayward girl. The gift that maybe Tano

passed on to you." The ultimate gift in the family, she said, the gift to the chosen ones was the ability to fly.

He had to laugh.

"Hush yu mout," she said. "Don't laugh at things you know nothing about. All the great ones know how to fly. Like Tano. In fact, once upon a time, all the ol' Africans that come here could fly. But once they touch ground, too many things happen to make them forget. Them foot stick too fast in the snare that set for them. Only a few, the few that remain faithful and true, could still fly back."

"Fly back where?"

"To Guinea."

"YaYa!"

"That is just what they call it, but is really the place where you meet again with the loved ones who leave you behind, the ones we call Ol' People. Ol' People turn into spirit already and spirit don't touch salt. In the old days, only the ones who don't touch salt could fly."

"That rules me out then," he said smiling weakly, humouring her.

"In this modern age, is hard to keep strictly to the rules."

"YaYa, this is a serious matter. You just can't bend the rules to suit yourself!" he burst out, genuinely shocked.

"Look at you, how little you weigh," she said, feeling his ribcage, lifting up one of his arms for exhibition, and laughing. "You like a little bird. You don't think yu getting ready to fly?"

He laughed, loudly this time, his laughter turning into a cough. By the time she brought him a drink, her mood had changed. She seemed angry.

"You don't have to believe. But I know what I know," she said as she turned down the lamp and left him.

His shoulder blades started to itch.

11

The next morning he woke up feeling too ill to get out of bed. In the evening, the old men arrived as they did every night now. Bro Nebo and Bro Samuel, his grandmother's friends. They came into his room and greeted him gently, scrutinizing him, before shyly touching their caps and retreating to the veranda. Tonight, he could hear their murmuring voices and that of YaYa seeming to come from very far away, coming and going, music that soothed. Later, YaYa came into the room with a small calabash full of a dark and viscous liquid. By now he had ceased to ask about anything she gave him and he swallowed it, trying not to gag.

"Jonathan, Brother Nebo bring this specially for you," she said. "It take a long time to make. Is not something to drink any and every day. We feel the time is ripe."

"For what?" he wanted to ask, but his senses were already fading.

"It will give you spirit. Whatever you are to be, will be."

12

He climbs into the forest-clad mountain. Thick creepers hanging from the trees entangle his every step, the bush of the under-growth tearing at his feet. He finds it hard going, but makes progress, hacking his way through with his machete, feeling strong. The forest is damp and cool, the way he has always known it to be. At first the task of cutting his way through is pleasant and he enjoys feeling his strength, but, as the day wears on, he begins to tire and sweat profusely. The trees seem to be moving farther and farther apart, allowing the full heat of the sun to pour down on his bare head. He is dying of heat and thirst and there is no water. He becomes tired and discouraged. He no longer bothers to look where he is going, though he continues to hack away. He cannot stop; he is impelled to go on, to what he has no idea.

Suddenly he is through the bush and into a clearing and it is so sudden and unexpected, his happiness so overwhelming, he starts to run. Blinded by the glare, by the sweat in his eyes, he fails to see what's ahead. Carried by his own momentum, he trips and falls into what he recognizes is an open grave. In that same instant, he sees himself lying in the grave. He is overcome by his terror, by horror, by the feeling of the fibres of his body dissolving, his bones flying apart. He comes to in a space that is empty and desolate; he knows it to be the place of death, of total aloneness, of total silence. He is scrabbling to hold on to the ground that is falling away but he cannot anchor himself. He is floating, floating up and up in the silent empty world with no sense of time until he sees emerging out of the blankness of the far distance a white mountain with deeply serrated edges. Standing on its summit is a woman, her head wrapped in red. As he comes closer to her, he sees she is extending both hands, imploring him to come. He understands this is where he is bound to go. He feels himself floating toward her as if flying, until he crashes head first into an invisible barrier. He plummets, stunned. He lifts himself pain-fully, and tries again to strive upwards, only to be beaten back. Though thrown down each time, he continues to struggle. The woman beckons, and he knows he has to crash through the barrier to float freely toward her, weightless, as if his body does not exist, his only sensation a dot of bitterness on his tongue that is spreading, from his tongue to the inside of his mouth and upward across his face, awakening each muscle by turn. His senses awaken too; he is hearing a sound, a kind of humming coming from the universe itself.

He opens his eyes to find Bro Nebo bending over him with a feather which he dips into a little calabash and applies a green liquid to his tongue. He feels the taste of it moving into his throat, spreading downward. Each capillary, each vein, each artery awakens as it is touched by the bitterness. As the sensation spreads throughout his body, like a slow-moving stream, each place touched by the liquid in its turn comes alive, not with a rush but slowly, like a counterpoint to that humming sound outside of himself that is coming and going, coming and going until his entire body is revived.

And in the very instant the last atom of his body is replaced, his tongue comes alive, uncontrolled. He is startled to hear what is pouring out of him in an endless stream; he hears himself giving voice to his most secret, his deadliest thoughts, his desires, his fears, narrating his every action, no matter how hidden, revealing even to himself his thoughts about his mother, his father, of all those he'd wronged, his wasted life. It all tumbles out, uncontrolled, his tongue a runaway train speaking of his illness, his battles with it, his distress, his fear of dying, finally naming it aloud, shouting its name, waiting for the echoes to come back, shouting it again, until the whole world is possessed by the sound which consumes everything and there is nothing left to say. He ceases to form sentences or words; he is reduced to babble, to retching and coughing up the remaining bits and pieces till finally he lies absolutely exhausted with nothing left to be expelled. Only then does Bro Nebo hold up his head and make him drink something that tastes like clear, fresh, pure water.

13

He comes awake in his bed and hears, faintly from the veranda, the humming and murmuring of his grandmother and the old men coming and going, before he falls into a deep, refreshing sleep.

14

He awakens next morning with the feeling that something momentous took place during the night, something that involved him. What, he has no idea.

His grandmother enters with a basin and a washcloth and no expression on her face.

"YaYa, what happened last night?"

"Nothing, mi son." She carefully puts the basin and the washcloth on the bedside table and leaves.

Jonathan turns his face to the wall and watches a line of ants. Something comes in a blinding flash: he knows what it is now, knows what he lost so many years ago as a child. The morning after the incident down by the river, he had awakened with a precious gift: the gift of understanding animals. He is sure now, sure that he had looked at the ants and had understood their every word, and he realized this was the source of his ability to predict. The animals had told him. He saw the day he stood on the road with his grandmother, and Sawyer and Thomas walked by. A bird in a branch above had looked him straight in the eye and said, "Poor Thomas, what a sorry day today," and he had his vision of the tree falling. That was what had made him scream out, "Thomas, don't go."

Lying in bed now, he remembers. He recalls how the gift had seemed so natural and ordinary, it never occurred to him to tell anyone. How after his long sleep, YaYa had teased him and asked him what had happened, and he had taken his mug of cocoa from her and said, "Nothing." He recalls the so-called predictions that had come through this gift, and how the morning after spending time with the priest, he had awakened to a sense of utter desolation.

He had been shut out from a place of unsullied joy. The door into enchantment, into companionship, had briefly opened and then cruelly slammed shut. He had fallen into nothingness.

Some of that devastation washes over him now. Here he is twenty years later and the ants on the wall still talk to each other but he overhears nothing, and the bird outside his window might be chattering in Greek for all he understands it. And it comes to him that YaYa too needed to be released from the burden of suffering she had carried most of her life, her own sense of loss – that he had been sent to fill the emptiness in her life just as she had relieved him of his.

He senses that she knows, as he does, that they are almost at the

end of the story. All that is left is to find out exactly what happened
by the river that day. For it was there he had received his gifts. He
runs through his mind the story his mother has told him, how
each day he would go and search for the most perfect fruit he
could find. Had he found something else that day? He looks
outside. "Come, come," the bird seems to be saying through the
window. "Yes, go," the ants seem to be urging. His shoulder
blades itch and the whole world feels as if it is stirring, alive with
sounds he has never heard before.

15

Jonathan feels surprisingly strong as he gets out of bed, pulls on
his shorts and a shirt and sandals and walks into the kitchen.

"YaYa," he says, "I am going down to the river."

She doesn't seem surprised. She hugs him tightly, then lets
him go. "Walk good," she says.

He takes the walking stick he has been using and starts his slow
descent to the river. Because of the drought, his every step
dislodges earth and stones which roll down the hill ahead of him
like heralds. This is the first time he has found the strength to
walk to this place, though he had wanted to do so from the very
start of his visit. He finds it bears no resemblance to what he had
imagined. It is parched like the rest of the land; instead of water,
the riverbed is nothing but a dry gully filled with stones. The lush
grove of guava and underbrush is gone, in its place a few straggling
trees bearing hard green fruit, some blackened on the tree, the few
ripened ones studded with worm holes.

But he doesn't feel discouraged. Something is there waiting
for him, just like the first time, something pulling him on,
wanting to be found. And since he doesn't know what really
happened the first time, he starts his search for the perfect guava.

He sees no sign of it on any of the nearby trees, but as he walks
on the bankside, the golden glow of one, high on a tree further
down the gully, beckons him. He turns back for one last look up

at the house and sees his grandmother standing on the hilltop, silhouetted against the skyline, hand shading her eyes from the sun. He waves, but she does not see him; she appears to be looking at something in the sky. She vanishes from view as he takes the plunge deeper into the gully.

The thought comes that she never told him how she knew that people with the gift could fly. For if they could fly, wouldn't they simply take off and never return? How could anyone know what had actually taken place? He remembers his grandmother telling stories of Tano's grand funeral, saying nothing of when Tano had flown. But by the time he has pushed farther up the gully bank the thought has slipped away, like his body, which seems to be dissolving, leaving him light and carefree as a child.

He gets nearer to where he thinks he has seen the guava and is surprised not to find it on that tree, though he immediately catches a glimpse of it farther on. He is not sure it is the same fruit – this one seems to be bigger and glowing, more inviting. He pushes on, feeling the excitement of chasing the object of his desire that is now, finally, within reach.

He plucks the guava from the tree and examines it closely. It is the most perfect fruit he has ever seen. Before he bites into it, it floods his senses with its fragrance; his ears come alive with the buzz and murmur of the universe. He is not surprised to see perched on the branch above his head the bird that has been outside his window, the same bird, he is sure, from his childhood.

He takes the first bite of the guava and chews very slowly, savouring it, the first solid food he has eaten in days. He happens to be facing the hills and, after a few bites, notices without surprise that they are becoming transparent, until he is able to see right through them into the other hills beyond and on to the highest mountain range. Above those, he sees the rain clouds assembling, can almost feel the drops on his face, hear the floodwater drumming down the gully, see the jubilant dance of Rivermaid triumphantly entering his grandmother's church to possess her followers.

A feeling of lassitude, of contentment, of great joy begins to steal over him as he consumes the fruit. When he comes to the last piece, he holds it in his hand for a very long time as if contemplating a final and irrevocable step. He feels a momentary twinge of regret as he pauses with the fruit halfway to his mouth.

It is then he becomes aware that out of all the sounds, one has clearly emerged, insistently demanding his attention. He looks up and recognizes it as the voice of the bird, a voice that must have been speaking to him for some time, for it is rather irritable and scolding, like that of a cranky old woman. He chews and swallows the last piece of guava and feels uplifted, as if he has sprouted wings. He laughs, for he realizes he clearly understands every word the bird is saying.

It is urging him. "Hurry up. Rain is coming. Let's go."

ACKNOWLEDGEMENTS

I am grateful to the editors of the following publications in which earlier versions of these stories appeared. All have been revised for this collection, some extensively. "The Pain Tree" was commissioned by cbc Radio for broadcast in the short story festival "Between the Covers"; first broadcast May 19, 1998 (read by Honor Ford-Smith) and subsequently published in *Caribbean Quarterly, Calabash* and *Stories from Blue Latitudes;* "Moonlight" in *Mangrove;* "Silent" in *Tell Tales Anthology, IV;* "A Father Like That" in *Kunapipi;* "Coal" in *Tongues of the Ocean ;* "Lollipop" in *tok 1: Writing the New Toronto;* "Boxed-In" in *Maple Tree Literary Supplement;* "Flying" in *Obsidian iii,* and *Maple Tree Literary Supplement* (mtls online).

I cannot at this stage name all the friends who have read and made useful suggestions to improve these stories over the years, but I hope they will find my gratitude expressed in this final version.

Thanks to the publisher of the Canadian edition, Cormorant Books, Marc Côté, and to Bryan Ibeas and the rest of the staff for their caring approach to publishing, and to Peepal Tree for this new edition. And thanks, as ever, to my agent Daphne Hart.

I am also grateful for an Ontario Arts Council grant from the Writers' Reserve.

ABOUT THE AUTHOR

Olive Senior is the prizewinning author of 17 books of fiction, poetry, non-fiction and children's literature. Born and brought up in Jamaica, she now lives in Canada. The Caribbean nevertheless remains the focus of her work and *The Pain Tree* recently won the overall 2016 OCM Bocas Prize for Caribbean literature. In 2015, she won the OCM Bocas non-fiction prize for *Dying to Better Themselves: West Indians and the Building of the Panama Canal*, a retelling of one of the greatest feats of engineering from a largely unknown perspective.

Her many other awards include the first Commonwealth Writers Prize (for her book *Summer Lightning*) and the Musgrave gold medal of the Institute of Jamaica for her contribution to Jamaican heritage. Her poetry book *Over the Roofs of the World* was a finalist for Canada's Governor-General's Award and her children's book *Anna Carries Water* is among the 20 books recommended by New York City Reads 365 for grade 1.

Her work is taught internationally and her poetry book *Gardening in the Tropics* is currently on the CAPE syllabus for Caribbean schools. She can be heard reading her poetry on the Poetry Archive http://www.poetryarchive.org. She is the subject of the book *Olive Senior* by Denise deCaires Narain in the Writers and their Work series, UK: Northcote Publishers 2011.

She lectures and conducts writing workshops internationally and is on the faculty of the Humber School for Writers, Humber College, Toronto.

www.olivesenior.com